I0733281

Two Murders
Too Many

———

By Bluette Matthey

Blue Shutter Publishing

Two Murders Too Many

Author: Bluette Matthey

This book is a work of fiction. Names, characters, places, and incidents are products of the author's imagination or are used fictitiously. Any resemblance to actual events or locales, or persons, living or dead, is entirely coincidental.

Copyright © 2020 by Blue Shutter Publishing

This book is licensed for your personal enjoyment only. This book may not be resold or given away to other people. All rights are reserved, including the right to reproduce this book or portions thereof in any form whatsoever. Thank you for respecting the hard work of this author.

Library of Congress control number on file with publisher.
ISBN: 978-1-941611-17-3

Other books by Bluette Matthey

From the Hardy Durkin Travel Mystery Series:

Corsican Justice
Abruzzo Intrigue
Black Forest Reckoning
Dalmatian Traffick
Engadine Aerie

Dedication

I grew up listening to the memories of my father's youth. Being an excellent storyteller, he crafted these recollections into captivating tales heard many times over but never too often.

To my father, Rolland Stratton, who was a masterful raconteur.

Map of Shannon

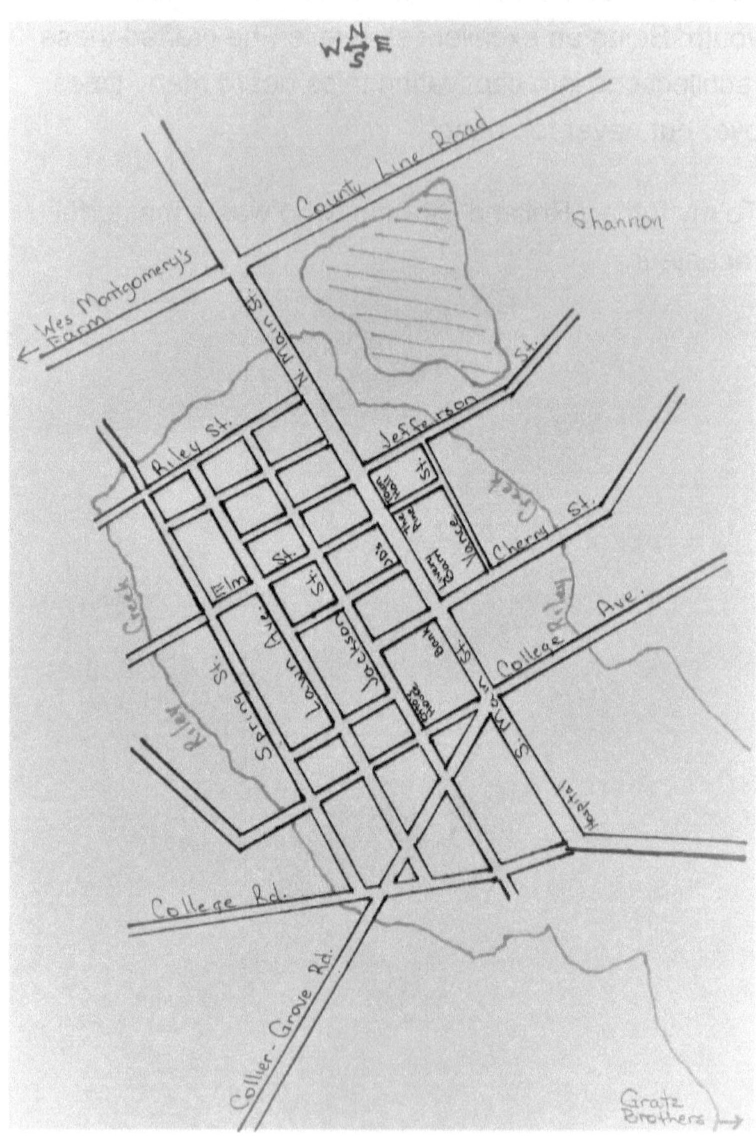

Prologue

When Charlie Simmons steps up as the new policeman in the close-knit community of Shannon he is not expecting a shocking, grisly murder to follow.

Charlie soon discovers the murdered victim, a local postman, also ran a lucrative blackmail enterprise, his list of victims in the *Who's Who* in Shannon and all with something to hide.

As Charlie masterfully untangles this network of extortion, a local wife comes up missing. Did she run away from an abusive husband, or is there a second victim somewhere?

Chapter One

Ding, dong, bell,
Pussy's in the well.
Who put her in?
Little Johnny Flynn.
Who pulled her out?
Little Tommy Stout.

---English nursery rhyme

From a distance the red-yellow glow of the fire consuming Clyde Gratz' barn looked warmly inviting on this chilly autumn night. Up close, however, it was heartbreaking to see. The old bank barn, built with local virgin timber more than a hundred years ago using eight-inch wooden pegs to brace the major joists together, creaked, groaned, and cracked loudly as the fire devoured the old wood. When the haymow caught fire and the bales of straw bedding started to burn, clouds of sparks rained down on the fire fighters or were carried off by the slight breeze.

The livestock, mercifully, had been freed from the inferno by Clyde's wife of twenty years, Miss Jenny. She had penned them up in the corn crib, which was empty since the corn was still on the `shock in the fields. Frightened baa's and belligerent moo's wafted over the night air, adding to the tragic spectacle.

"Hey, Uncle Charlie!" Rolland Simmons called, arriving at the scene on his red and black Chief bicycle from Sears that was his pride and joy. The bike's black leather seat, matching leather tool bag, and rubber block pedals were all embossed

with the 'Chief' logo. It was the newest 1956 model. The
neatest thing about Rolland's bike, he thought, was the oval-
shaped head badge decorating the front of the bike. It showed
a profile of an Indian chief's head in full regalia, and it was cast
in bronze with cloisonné-colored glass giving brilliance to the
chief's head dress.

Rolland Simmons was a popular high school senior in
Shannon. He played the position of right tackle on the football
team, enjoyed public speaking, and excelled at mechanical
drawing. He lived with his Aunt Emily since his stepmother, a
cold woman, was an ever-painful reminder of the loving
mother he had lost to an infection during the childbirth of a
sibling who later died, as well.

Uncle Charlie turned when he heard his name called. He was a
member of the Shannon Volunteer Fire Brigade and fighting
the barn fire had left him sweaty and covered in soot. The
once-white thermal underwear shirt he wore was now streaked
with black and full of tiny holes from the cascades of sparks
spewed out by the fire.

"Why Rolland, what are you doing out this time of night? Does
Emily know you're here?"

Rolland grinned hugely. "Aw, Charlie, it's Saturday night. I'm
'llowed to stay up late on Saturdays."

Sweat ran down Charlie's face in runnels. The fierce heat from
the blaze was pushing the firemen back as the fire gained the
upper hand.

"Ya gonna be able to save Clyde's barn? Rolland asked.

His answer came when the barn's roof caved in with a giant whoosh and a roar, sending an enormous, thick torrent of sparks skyward as the fire intensified. The hungry flames reached fifty feet in the air. Rolland sat on his bike, somberly watching the death throes of the burning barn. He knew what losing a barn meant to a farmer in the farming community of Shannon, Ohio. Especially going into winter, when the animals had to be housed out of the bitter cold and damp.

Charlie's shoulders slumped in defeat and fatigue; the battle was lost. The structure would burn itself out, eventually. All the firemen could do now was see that it did not spread to other buildings or threaten any trees or crops that were still in the nearby fields. It would be a long night; he hoped Miss Jenny would make some sandwiches and strong coffee.

*****

The small mid-Western town of Shannon was abuzz the next morning with news of the barn fire, and gawkers and concerned neighbors stopped by the Gratz place, just south of town, to stare at the loss and gather snippets of gossip, or offer condolences and promises to help with a new barn before winter set in. For perhaps the tenth time that morning Clyde had recited his movements of the night before and the events following the discovery of the fire.

"It was Saturday night, Town Night," he told his neighbors. "Tom, my brother, and me was chewing the fat with some of the regular guys at Bott's Hardware, like we do every Saturday evenin'. We was sittin' in the back of the store, in Henny's office, when Sankie Fenton ran in and shouted that my barn was on fire and we'd better come quick.

11

"Tom drove me home and by the time we got here Jenny had saved the animals. We'd just baled straw this past week and stacked it in the mow, so all that's lost. Didn't lose any equipment. The tractors and corn picker were over by the corn crib, so at least I'll be able to get the crop picked. What with the animals using the corn crib I don't know where I'll put the corn's, the problem."

"You can store your corn at my place," Wilbur Steiner offered. "I've got an empty crib you can use 'till you get things sorted out."

Clyde nodded his thanks. "I appreciate that, Wilbur," he said.

"We'll get a barn up for ya, too, Clyde, before cold weather comes," Hikey Huber told him. "Give us a few weeks to finish gettin' our crops off and stored and we'll get to it."

Clyde was more than a little relieved, as well as touched by the goodness of his neighbors in his predicament. Shannon was a close-knit community, and everybody kind of looked after everybody else. He would be able to repay everyone when the insurance company came through for his loss.

The remainder of the week passed with the local farmers busy harvesting the rest of the soybeans, and then starting in on the fields of corn that blanketed the flat farmland for miles and miles around the village. The loss of the Gratz barn was not forgotten, but the memory of the fire had woven itself into the fabric of the community and had been somewhat muted by the everyday routine of rural small-town life.

*****

Chapter Two

For its very modest size, the village of Shannon had a disproportionately large number of town characters who were generally visible on a day-to-day basis on the sidewalks of Shannon. Some were simple-minded, and some were just plain ornery. Times were easier and gentler, socially, and these notables roamed the village freely. They were not harmed, nor were they feared of doing harm.

One theory for such a plethora of characters is that the Swiss settlement that was founded on the western perimeter of Shannon had kept pretty much to itself. In the early days, the settlement had its own blacksmiths, barbers, and watch repair shops. Most of the settlement's social activity centered around the church, and new bloodlines infused into the small community were rare.

The town was full of Dillers, Luginbuhls, Badertschers, Reichenbachs, Augsburgers, Buchers, et al. whose ancestors had first settled in the Swiss community. After a time, cousins started marrying cousins. The incidences of inbreeding resulted in the occasional mental deviant. Sometimes, the end-result of such inter-marrying yielded an extremely gifted, intelligent progeny, but more often the result of tying the bloodlines too closely produced what was at the time called a 'soft head'.

Often freakishly deformed, the more seriously impaired idiots were kept on the family farm, out of the public eye and harm's way. The milder cases were able to live close to normal lives, coming and going like everyone else. They were well known to the public at large and were accepted and looked after by the wider community.

One such member of the community was a young man in his late twenties called Luke McGluke. Luke washed and waxed new cars for the Ford garage and showroom and referred to himself as the 'Simonize King.' He would hang out on Main Street when he wasn't simonizing and could often be found lounging on the sidewalk bench in front of the Presbyterian Church. One of Luke's contemporaries, Sammy Habegger, would sit with Luke and on more than one occasion a jawing match would ensue, with Sammy taking the superior mental position.

"I'm nuts and know it, and you're nuts and don't know it," Sammy would say, smugly, as if that made Luke more an idiot than Sammy.

Pushed past his limit, Luke would lunge at his tormenter, and a scuffle would break out with the young men rolling around on the church lawn. It would be the task of whoever happened to be passing by to break it up, and if it happened to be Old Miss McKebben with her pointed umbrella things got sorted quickly. She was liberal with her jabs and swats and did not take such foolishness lightly.

"You'll be a-peeking through the pearly gates, Luke McGluke," she'd warn. "And not let in on account of such heathen goings-on. And as for you, Sammy Habegger," she'd say, rolling her eyes, "well, I never!" And then she would deliver one final, insidious jab.

The boys would look suitably penitent, heads hanging, and Old Miss McKebben, thus mollified by their contrition and satisfied she had done right by them both, would continue on her way with a heightened air of dignity. Her interventions always left the lads in a state of relief from her loathsome umbrella and united in their mutual deliverance. That's just how things were in Shannon.

*****

Chapter Three

Police Chief Pete Gaite decided to call round to Jo Dale's Cully's house the Tuesday morning after Clyde Gratz's barn burned in the hopes that he might have some information about the recent barn fire in Shannon. Joe Dale was one of Shannon's town characters who always seemed to know what was going on in that special way that town characters do. They had their own network of oddball acquaintances that forever has an ear to the ground. Chief Gaite thought of them as the Shannon Irregulars, though they were woefully incomparable to Sherlock Holmes' gang of urchins in 19th century London.

Jo Dale Cully was a big man. He had a huge square head, raven-black hair that he wore longer than most men, and a face whose skin was always smooth as a baby's bottom. It was said that he was part Indian. He also wasn't quite right in the head.

His mom knew he was a few corners short of a square when he was little, so she had something done to him so he wouldn't ever bother anyone. And he never did. Bother anyone. He used to wander into peoples' houses and snoop in cupboards and drawers, but he never stole anything or threatened anyone. In fact, he was always real polite to people, calling them 'Mister So-and-So' or 'Mrs. So-and-So.'

He invariably looked down as he walked, looking for money someone might have dropped. He had a peculiar gait to his walk. Since he searched the pavement Tnent as he walked his shoulders were slightly hunched forward, and he rolled off his right foot. Not nearly a lurch; more like a slight limp.

Jo Dale always wore blue jean pants and a blue jean jacket buttoned clear up to his neck, no matter how hot it was outside. His jean pants were not like the Levis or Lees you bought in the store; Jo Dale's jeans looked home-made.

Jo Dale invariably smelled like soap. For years he worked in a laundry in nearby Lima, Ohio, and he handled washing powder all day, so his clothes absolutely reeked of soap. It covered up for the fact that he didn't bathe regularly. Say what you will about Jo Dale, he was never on welfare.

It was raining pretty hard when Pete pulled up to the curb in front of Jo Dale's house, which was located on Main Street, just two doors down from the corner of Jefferson and Main. Pete donned a rain slicker, snugged his chief's hat on his head, and hurried to the front stoop of the Cully home. He knocked on the front door.

The old house was in need of work, he noticed. Was it him, or was the house leaning to one side? The eaves were full of leaves and twigs that had been there long enough to sprout. The asbestos siding was cracking in places, and some pieces had fallen off and lay on the ground next to the foundation.

It was sad to see the place in such disrepair. Jo Dale's momma, Margaret Cully, had been a simple but good woman who had lived in Shannon all her life. She had raised Jo Dale and his two older brothers, both now living out of state somewhere. Margaret had been dead and gone for more than ten years, and Jo Dale lived in the old house alone.

He and his momma had had a close relationship. Margaret was, understandably, protective of her youngest and most vulnerable child. Jo Dale had always helped with the large vegetable garden Margaret put out every spring, and he was often seen walking the railroad ties of the local spur for the berry bushes that grew up alongside the tracks.

Jo Dale had run across the Weinhold sisters picking black berries near the town power plant one afternoon in late June and told them to git. "Them's my berries," he told them. He was very possessive of what he called 'his' berry patches scattered around town.

The door creaked open. "Mr. Police Chief," Jo Dale said. His smooth-skinned face never registered any expression. "It's raining."

"Yes, Jo Dale, it sure as hell is," Pete assured him. "Mind if I come in?"

Jo Dale stepped back, opening the door wide for Chief Gaite to enter.

"What the hell …" Pete said, his mouth gaped open.

Water dripped down from the living room ceiling in at least a dozen places. A collection of cans, pans, and pots were strategically placed to catch all the drips. The cacophony of plinks and plunks made by the drips was almost musical. It wasn't the noise that confounded Chief Gaite, though. It was the tent Jo Dale had pitched in the middle of the living room into which he now invited the chief so they could get out of the rain inside his house.

"How long you been living like this?" the police chief asked.

Jo Dale shrugged.

"Why, this house should be condemned," Chief Gaite said.

"Got no place else to go," Jo Dale pointed out.

Chief Gaite started to say something, but realized he had nothing to say, so he said nothing about Jo Dale's house. He remembered why he had stopped by in the first place.

"Ah, Jo Dale, you hear about the barn burnin' this past week?"

Jo Dale nodded.

"You get about. You know anything about the fire? Hear or see anything suspicious?"

Jo Dale nodded. "I know exactly what burned that barn," he said.

"You do?" Chief Gaite asked.

The big Indian nodded again. "I do, Chief Gaite," he said. "I saw a UFO flyin' real low over Clyde's barn the other night. It flew past once just to get a look, then came back and shot his barn. I mean, a streak a fire like a lightnin' bolt shot outta that flyin' saucer and set that barn on fire so quick I just couldn't believe it."

Chief Gaite stood a moment, just looking at Jo Dale. He sighed, inwardly. He didn't know why he'd even bothered to stop by.

"Well, thanks Jo Dale, for that information," he managed. He ducked out of the tent and let himself out and felt like he had just had an out-of-body experience. He had asked for it, he supposed. He just wanted to get back to the police station and have a hot cup of coffee while he mulled over what to do about Jo Dale's house.

*****

Chapter Four

Charlie Simmons was waiting in the chief's office at the station when he arrived. Charlie Simmons worked in his brother Cliff's garage on Elm Street. He was an ace mechanic and had a head for figures, which meant he also helped Cliff with the books of the garage business. Charlie was the older of the two brothers, but in the garage, Cliff was the boss and Charlie respected that.

Charlie had also been sworn in as deputy to the police chief on a permanent basis, so he was privy to everything that went on in Shannon. He knew and was known by every single person who lived in the community. He and his wife, Faerie, never had any children, but all the kids and dogs in Shannon loved Charlie; he was that kind a guy. He always carried a handful of pennies in his pants pocket and as the kids crowded around him when they saw him on the sidewalk, he would dole out the pennies. They worshipped him for it.

He was not big in stature, but tales of his physical strength were part of his story. Charlie was five-feet-ten and tipped the scales at around 150 pounds, so not a lion of a man by any standards. But dynamite comes in small packages. It was said he could take a fifty-pound burlap sack of livestock feed in his teeth and swing the damned thing onto a buck wagon without using his hands …. just his teeth. You got to have a neck like a bull to do something like that.

Pete Gaite stomped his feet to shake off the rain and took off his rain slicker and shook it before draping it over a coat hook.

He knocked the water off his hat with the palm of his hand and perched it on his desktop.

"What can I do for you, Charlie?" Pete asked.

"You got any thoughts about Clyde's barn burnin'?" Charlie asked.

Pete pursed his lips and shook his head.

"No, Charlie," he said. "I sure as hell don't. I just stopped by Jo Dale Cully's place to see if he knew anything."

Charlie cracked a grin. He had known Jo Dale all his life. He didn't say anything; he just waited for Pete to continue.

"He's a fruit cake. He made up the damnedest story and really expected me to believe it. *He* believed it." Pete was shaking his head. "But that's not the worst of it," he went on. "You ever been in Jo Dale's house?"

Charlie's grin got wider, but he still said nothing.

"The house is full of leaks. Water dripping everywhere. He's pitched a tent in his living room and lives in that to get out of the rain in the house." Pete still could not get over what he'd seen. "He's camping out in his house, for heaven's sake! The place needs to be torn down. Cripes, what if he starts a campfire in there? I don't want to put the man out of his home, Charlie, but there's limits to what's illegal and dangerous, and his house is both."

"Well, Pete," Charlie said slowly, "if it was me, I'd call one of the deacons at the Mennonite or Methodist church and ask if they've got an indigent fund for helping people like Jo Dale.

See if they could send some carpenters or handymen by to patch things up in his house so it's livable. You can't go runnin' the man outta his house. Where would he go? He's got no earthly relatives 'round here that I know of. He's been in Shannon all his life. He's part of our town." Charlie shook his head. "No, Pete, you can't tear down the man's house, even though the town's been trying to do that for pretty near a decade or more."

Pete knew Charlie was right. He, Pete, was a relative newcomer to Shannon. He had arrived in town in 1941, fifteen years ago. The nation's economy was still in disarray even though the Great Depression had come to an end in the spring of 1933. Pete was looking for a place to call home after his life was upended by the loss of industrial jobs in Pittsburg, his home. He had experienced first-hand the deprivations of economic upheaval in a big city and wanted to live in the country where a person could at least grow his food if need be.

In Pittsburg, Pete had been night watchman for a plywood factory, but with the onset of the Depression people quit buying new homes, builders quit building new homes, and private construction came to a standstill. Pete's job loss was a casualty of this deep malaise, and he was unable to get work.

Pete was determined not to end up in a Hooverville, a ramshackle community of cardboard boxes, tents, and rickety wooden sheds inhabited by the homeless which grew up, overnight, on vacant lots. He had seen whole families reduced to complete squalor in these ghettos, visiting soup kitchens or begging for food to survive.

He had headed west, to Ohio's farm country. Life would be simpler, compared to the big city of Pittsburg. He reckoned, correctly, that life would also be healthier and the local people more accepting of a stranger. He passed through lots of farmland as he traveled. What captivated him about Shannon was that the local farmers were burning their corn crops as fuel because it was cheaper than coal, and the countryside surrounding the town smelled like popcorn. He took this as a sign and decided to stay.

Pete Gaite worked in Cliff Simmons' garage for well over a year after his arrival in the small Ohio town. Pete was not a mechanic, so Cliff paid him basic wages for the chores of a general dog's body …running errands, cleaning the shop, moving tires … anything to keep him busy.

Pete earned just enough to get by, and was thankful for it, but when the position of police chief opened up in Shannon Pete put his name forward for the job. Cliff was a well-respected citizen and merchant in Shannon, his family could count eight generations of Simmons in the area, and when he put in a good word for Pete to get the job as police chief, that's just what happened.

The pace of rural Shannon suited Pete just fine. He wasn't a particularly bright man, but his intellect seemed evenly matched to the level of crime committed in the small town: a speeding ticket here and there, now and then a domestic situation (usually alcohol was involved), and pranks played by college kids from Shannon College. Refreshingly routine and nothing Pete couldn't handle.   *****

Chapter Five

Aside from church activities, there was little social life for farmers around Shannon. Over a period of years, it had developed that Wednesday and Saturday nights were town nights for the men who farmed in the area, and Bott's Hardware was one of the favorite loafing spots in town.

There were two hardware stores in Shannon, both on Main Street within a block of each other. Bott's was bigger, brighter, and sold major appliances and housewares, as well as the usual hardware miscellany. Clarence Bott had started the retail business as a means of showcasing his cream separator to the local Shannon population, and then expanded the business to include a much larger inventory.

The farmers, the primary customers for his cream separator, took to meeting up at Bott's hardware while they were in town to share bits of news and gossip indigenous to the farming community around Shannon, and this initial meeting place, in time, developed into the Wednesday-night-Saturday-night meeting ritual. Several town men would show up from time to time, usually businessmen who serviced the farm community in some way.

Henny Bott had taken the hardware over from his dad after the old man retired. Henny was not as social as his dad had been, but he kept the town night tradition alive at the hardware; it was good for business and public relations. It was an oddity for farmers and town people to get on, and it was all on account of

Clarence's invention of the cream separator, which made the farmers' lives a whole lot simpler.

The men would gather around the coal-burning stove that warmed Henny's roomy office, sitting on an odd collection of old chairs and a dusty, threadbare sofa, trading stories, catching up on gossip, and offering rural points of view on all subjects. Several spittoons had been strategically placed around the sitting area, and it was not unusual for a bottle or two to be passed around among those present.

It was, truly, a man's world at Bott's on town nights. Even though the hardware closed its doors to business at nine o'clock at night, the men gathered in the rear of the store in Henny's office would sit and gab and trade stories until the wee hours of the morning sometimes, though the farmers usually left a good deal earlier since the farm chores wouldn't wait, even on a Sunday morning.

The Saturday night following the fire at Clyde Gratz' farm a robust group of locals had gathered in front of the stove, among them the Gratz brothers, one of the town's retired police chiefs, Warren Brauen, Charlie Simmons, Charlie's brothers Orton and Cliff Simmons, and Henny. The men and their families had been residents of Shannon and friends for generations, so there was an air of bonhomie as they visited. When the occasional customer wandered into the store Henny would excuse himself from the group and wait on him. Women never shopped at Bott's on Saturday night; it just wasn't done.

"You miss not bein' the police chief anymore, Warren?" Charlie asked.

Warren Brauen was a tough looking old guy, gruff in his ways. He had been Shannon's police chief for over two decades, but had retired, paving the way for his successor, Stoney Baker, to take over. Stoney had not lasted long due to health issues, and Pete Gaite became chief. Warren took a swig from a bottle of home-made applejack and wiped his mouth.

"Heaven's no," he said. There was a brief pause as the other men waited expectantly. They knew what was coming. "I ever tell you about the time I caught George Hersey a stealin' wheat?"

No one said anything; they weren't meant to. They all waited for Warren to continue.

"Years ago," he began, "there was a flour mill in town that made flour outta the wheat the farmers round town brought to the mill to sell. Our Sweet Home Flour, the flour was called. Anyways, the mill would buy wheat to fill up its storage bins and ship the excess wheat on to Cleveland by train. The mill here would weigh the wheat when it was loaded into the covered hopper car and the train car would be sealed, but when it arrived at the other end it would always be several bushels short. This shortage had been goin' on for a month or two, and no one could figure out what was causin' it. It had everyone here at the mill and the train folks in Cleveland rightly puzzled."

He paused a moment to spit, wiped his mouth, and then continued. "The mill manager told me when the next shipment would be a goin' out, so I hid in one of the buildings back a' the mill with the door cracked open so's I could see. The moon was out, full, and I could see like it was daylight. Along about midnight I hear someone splashing his way up the creek and wouldn't you know, it's George Hersey, wearin' gum boots, and he's got a canvas rolled up under his arm.

"Well, he crawls under the train car that's holdin' the wheat, rolls out the piece of canvas underneath it, and proceeds to drill a hole in the bottom of the car with a brace and bit he'd had wrapped up in the canvas. He proceeds to fill up three burlap bags he brought along with 'im with the wheat that's running out the hole he drilled, and when he's done he tamps a plug he brought with him into the hole to seal it, and ties off his bags of wheat.

"George was just startin' to head home with his wheat. I opened the door to where I was hiding to get a better look at things and the door squeaked. George heard me, dropped his wheat, and took off runnin' down the railroad tracks. There was no way I could catch that long-legged SOB, so I went down and waited in his barn. Right about daylight he comes home, peeking around the corner of his barn.

"C'mon, George," I says. "The jig's up." George threw his hands up, sayin', "Don't shoot!"'" Warren spit, again, and chuckled.

"He got a year in the penitentiary for that little trick." He thought a moment and continued. "There's a little preamble to that story. Back in the day there were about as many saloons in Shannon as there were churches, which created a good deal of enmity between the 'wets', those in favor of selling booze in town, and the 'drys', those who were opposed to alcohol in town, usually for religious reasons.

"Some of the 'wets' got to drinkin' one night and went out and burned a big barn on Henry Tirbaugh's farm. Henry was an influential voice for the 'drys.' They got caught, naturally, and ended up spending a year in the Ohio pen for it. This was Midge Tillman, and two others, I forget their names.

"Well, when he got out, Midge would be talkin' to somebody on the street uptown and George Hersey would be drivin' by in his spring wagon and he'd stop and call out to Midge, "Hey, Midge, how high's the walls down there?", meaning the walls in the penitentiary. He loved taunting Midge about his time in the pen and it made Midge madder 'n hell.

"So, years later, after George spent a year in the pen for his wheat stealin', he'd be driving by in his spring wagon and Midge would call out, "Hey, George!" And George would slow down, "What, Midge?" he'd say. And Midge would ask, "George, how high's the walls down there?" And George would reply, "A damn sight's higher than what you'd think! Giddap!""

Warren's expression sobered, and he shook his head. "George's son, Myron, is the reason I quit being police chief." He paused to spit. "I was patrolling the alleys behind the business district late one Friday, checking all the rear entrances to make sure they was locked. When I tried the back door to Steiner's Men's Store and found the door open I started down the steps to see what was up and that fool, Myron, who was hiding down below, took a shot at me. Bullet glanced off the cement wall a foot from my head."

He spat, again. "Course, at the time I didn't know it was Myron. Anyhow, he managed to get by me and led me on a merry chase around Shannon's alleys for pertinear forty minutes until I saw who it was.

"Myron," I called out, "I know it's you, Son. Just throw down the gun and let's call it a day."

"And that's what he did," Warren said. "He didn't do time in the pen for that stunt, but he got into some serious trouble after he moved to Columbus. Far's I know he's still locked up." He shook his head. "Bad seed," Warren said. "That incident convinced me it was time to hang up my spurs."

It wasn't the first time the men had listened to Warren's tale, nor would it be the last. Warren had a knack for telling a good story and sitting around the coal stove in Bott's on a town night was the perfect place to hear them.

Just then Sankie Fenton threw open the door. "Is Tom Gratz in here?" he shouted.

 Somewhere along the way Sankie had assumed the role of town crier. With a perpetual cowlick in his dark hair he was an adult dead ringer for the Little Rascal's character of Alfalfa. His christened name was Arthur, but he had been called Sankie for as far back as anybody could remember.

Sankie was twenty-four years old and a fixture on the streets of Shannon. He was just soft-headed enough that he could not keep a job, but well able to function socially while continuing to live with his parents. The only noticeable trait that Sankie was a bit short of a dozen, mentally, was his wide-set hazel eyes that seemed to have a hard time focusing. That, and the fact that he was easily excitable and had to often be calmed down by the nearest adult. His normal speaking voice was a shout.

"I'm here!" Tom responded, rising from his chair.

"Come quick, Tom! Your barn's a burnin'!"

One barn burning might be an accident, but when the second Gratz barn caught fire, Shannon was set ablaze with suspicion and fear.

*****

Chapter Six

The Pine restaurant had been a fixture in Shannon for decades. It was located on Main Street two doors down from town hall. An alley ran along the side of The Pine, separating it from a recent competitor that had opened up across the alley.

The Pine restaurant occupied the entire ground floor of the Simmons Building. A long stairwell, accessed by a single door to the right of the restaurant's entrance, led up to the second floor of the building that had been made over into apartments which ran the depth of the building by means of a long, meandering hallway. The entire vast area on the right-hand side of this hall was a single, large apartment that housed the Rachler family who owned and ran The Pine. The apartments on the left of the hall were one-bedroom units rented out to single men working in Shannon.

Another door, to the right of the stairwell entrance, was the entryway to the Eight Ball Bar and Pool Room. To the right of the pool room's door was the entrance to Shalley's five-and-dime. All the businesses were in the Simmons Building, now owned by the Rachler family. In addition to the income from The Pine and the apartments, Jim Rachler made a decent monthly income from leasing to these other businesses.

One enormous, plate-glass window that ran almost floor to ceiling across the restaurant's front was emblazoned with "The Pine Restaurant," and allowed passersby on the sidewalk to see who was in the restaurant. The restaurant was not an official loafing spot in Shannon, but it was definitely a favorite meeting place, especially after local sporting events.

The Pine served home-cooked food but was famous for its grill menu. The Tall Pine Burger was a favorite, featuring generous, double hamburger patties, cheese, lettuce, and tomato with a mayonnaise/mustard dressing, held together by an extra-long toothpick with a squiggle of green cellophane at its top that was supposed to look like a pine tree.

The other big draw for The Pine restaurant was the pies it sold. Aunt Ethel, for years, had risen at four in the morning to bake pies for her brother's, Jim Rachler's, restaurant. Every day, without fail, Aunt Ethel rolled out pie crusts for two dozen pies in a plethora of flavors that the citizens of Shannon readily consumed and appreciated. Then she would head home and go back to bed, often reappearing in mid-afternoon in case the pies were selling out too quickly.

Chief Gaite was drinking coffee and eating a piece of banana cream pie in The Pine on the Wednesday morning after the second barn burned when another of Shannon's town characters stopped in for breakfast.

Dewey Fordham had wandered into Shannon shortly before World War II began. One day he was just there. No one saw him get off the bus and he did not have a car, so it was assumed he walked or hitched a ride. He was a peculiar, diminutive man in his forties who shuffled when he walked. He walked everywhere, carrying a cane and smoking a corn cob pipe. When he sucked on his pipe his cheeks collapsed inward; Dewey didn't have many teeth.

He had done odd jobs around Shannon for many years, including being the night watchman at the local IGA grocery store. He guarded the store's watermelons, left outside the in a large bin overnight, and anything else that could be carried off under dark of night. Eventually, the town fathers decided he was an OK guy and offered him work, but he kept his job at the IGA.

The town gave Dewey a job guarding Shannon's trash dump. Shannon put an old, small house trailer off to one side inside the fenced-in dump area, and that's where Dewey lived. His trailer did not have running water, but the town did manage to hook up electricity. It was free, and the arrangement suited Dewey just fine.

He wore blue jeans and a blue jean jacket like Jo Dale, except Dewey's jeans were Lees and they did not smell like soap powder. He would wear his jeans and matching jacket until they practically walked on their own, they were so stiff with dirt, then he would throw them away and buy a new set. Folks in town got to calling him Dirty Doc, which was, affectionately, shortened to just Doc.

Doc took his job of guarding the town dump very seriously and enforced the policy that only residents of Shannon could haul trash to the dump. This did not sit well with the farmers, who paid taxes to the town and bought all their goods in Shannon. They thought they should be able to use the dump, too, but Doc was adamant.

You would see Dewey walking up town every morning about 8:30 heading to The Pine restaurant for a complimentary breakfast. Local farmers knew his schedule and used his mealtimes as a window of opportunity to haul all the aluminum cans and other trash they had collected over a six-month period to the dump. Doc never figured it out, and everybody was happy.

"Mornin', Doc," Chief Gaite said.

Dewey took his pipe out of his mouth and nodded. He took one of the stools at the counter, leaning his cane against the laminate surface. The man sitting two stools down casually got up and moved to a table ten feet away. Sitting down wind from Doc could ruin your appetite.

Rolland Simmons, acting as grill boy, sauntered up to Doc on the other side of the counter. Rolland started working for his great uncle, Big Jim Rachler, at The Pine restaurant when he turned sixteen. At first, Rolland worked in the kitchen as a dish washer, but he was restless and always looking for more work to do so he was taught how to run the grill. That suited Rolland just fine. His new position not only earned him more money, but he was up in the front of the restaurant with the customers and privy to all the gossip and breaking news that floated around the restaurant.

"Hey, Doc. The usual?" he asked.

Doc gave a nod. Two poached eggs, order of toast and jam, hot black coffee, and a piece of pie. He was a man of few words. Some folks thought he was simple, but his dark, quick eyes said otherwise. The truth about Dewey Fordham, which no one in Shannon knew, was that he had had a tragic and traumatic childhood which left him almost devoid of emotion. His aloofness was his defense mechanism. He didn't know that, but that's what it was, and it enabled Doc to close off most of his life from sorrow, shame, and humiliation.

After Doc finished his eggs and toast, he asked Rolland, "What kind a pie ya got today, Rolland?" It was a ritual question Doc asked every day. He loved hearing Rolland recite the litany of pies The Pine restaurant offered.

"Why Doc, we've got apple, cherry, peach, banana cream, pecan, pineapple, coconut, strawberry, blueberry, blackberry, chocolate, butterscotch, rhubarb, molasses, custard, and raisin cream," Rolland replied, in one long breath.

Doc nodded. "I believe I'll have blueberry today, Rolland."

Rolland grinned. Doc had blueberry pie every day of his life.

"Sure, Doc," he said. "Comin' right up."

His pie eaten, Doc collected his cane and pipe to head back to his trailer.

"Hey, Doc," Chief Gaite said as Doc walked by, "You know or hear anything about the Gratz brothers' barns burning?"

Several heads of patrons in the restaurant turned toward Doc, and Rolland pretended to be busily cleaning the counter next to where Doc stood, all listening for his reply. Typical for Doc, his response was slow in coming. He sucked in on his pipe, which had gone out, so he took it out of his mouth and gave it an annoyed look before palming it in the Captain Kangeroo pocket of his denim jacket.

"Don't know nuthin 'bout that," he finally said. *****

Chapter Seven

On the Thursday after the second Gratz brother's barn burned Police Chief Pete Gaite had gone to Detroit, Michigan, to visit his older sister who was ailing. Charlie took over as acting Police Chief in his absence. Pete hated to leave with the Gratz brothers' situation unresolved but Lila, his sister, lived alone and he was all she had. He figured not much would change in the three weeks he would be gone, and he would deal with it all when he returned. All Charlie had to do was tread water with things until he got back.

There had been no new developments on the barn burnings, and although the incidents were far from forgotten they had been put on the back burner of everyone's mind, for the most part. Except for Charlie. He continued to question Doc, Sankie Fenton, and even Luke McGluke, who was uptown all hours of the day and night, but nobody knew anything.

Charlie stopped by The Pine on Thursday morning for a cup of coffee and a piece of Aunt Ethel's butterscotch pie and, when he left, he exited out the side door that opened on the alley. He walked toward the back of the restaurant and was transfixed by what he heard.

"Yea, though I walk through the valley of the shadow of death I will fear no evil: for Thou art with me; Thy rod and Thy staff they comfort me," a strong, deep voice intoned.

Then a second, slurring, voice chimed in: "For whosoever shall call upon the name of the Lord shall be saved."

Charlie came around the back of The Pine just in time to see Lazarus Bassinger (nicknamed Lottsie) take a swig from a whisky jug he and Fred Birknauer were sharing. Both men were seated on the ground of the empty lot behind the restaurant under a big elm tree quoting scripture to one another. Fred had gone to seminary as a young man, but never finished. Instead, he had returned to Shannon and become a paper hanger for a one-man wallpaper business that barely fed his family.

Lazarus held up his right hand. "How about this one: 'For all who are led by the Spirit of God are Sons of God.'"

Fred listened somberly, a rapt expression on his face. Both men were completely pie-eyed, and it wasn't even noon yet.

"Wine is a mocker, strong drink is raging: and whosoever is deceived thereby is not wise," Charlie quoted.

Fred and Lazarus turned their bleary eyes to where Charlie stood. Fred's face broke into a toothy grin. "Charlie!" He vaguely motioned for Charlie to join them. Lottsie held up the jug, offering him a drink.

"Where in the hell did you boys get a jug this early in the day?" he asked. Just then Rolland Simmons arrived, slightly out of breath.

"Uncle Charlie," Rolland said by way of greeting.

"Hey Rolland," Charlie replied. "You're not joining these two, are you?"

"Nah. Aunt Agnes sent me to bring Uncle Fred home and put him to bed." Rolland bent down and gave Fred his hand.

"C'mon Uncle Fred," he said. "Agnes says it's time for you to git on home."

Lottsie laid his index finger on the side of his nose and winked. "Yer woman's not happy with ya, Fred," he said, grinning.

Fred mumbled something under his breath and took Rolland's hand to be helped up. Fred had lost a leg in an automobile accident several years earlier and his wooden stump made maneuvering difficult, but Rolland got him upright and started him toward home, half carrying him.

Charlie watched the pair go, a smile playing on his lips. He knew Big Agnes, Fred's wife, and could only imagine what lay in store for Fred once he was home.

He turned his attention back to Lottsie. In his late fifties, Lazarus was a retired bricklayer who liked to tip the bottle occasionally. He had a big white beard, large stomach, and merry disposition. He lived in a little house covered in green tar paper on the bend of Riley Creek, and all the kids in town called him Santa Claus. His genial face was perpetually red, whether from drink or being out of doors a lot.

"Lazarus, you hear anything about the fires that took out the Gratz brothers' barns?"

Lottsie shook his big head.

"You see anything or anybody unusual at all around town?"

Lottsie thought a moment. "Well, I seen that Cooper fella from Rawson hanging out the back door of the Eight Ball," he said, referring to the pool room adjacent The Pine. It harbored some unsavory characters from time to time.

"When was this?" Charlie asked.

Lottsie scrunched his face in thought. "Dunno for sure, but I think it was a week ago this past Monday."

"What do you know about this Cooper, Lazarus?"

Lottsie took a short pull on his jug and wiped his mouth with the back of his hand. "Only that he's meaner n' a snake," he said. "If looks could kill the streets would be littered with bodies from his evil eye. 'And if thine eye offend thee, pluck it out, and cast it from thee: it is better for thee to enter into life with one eye, rather than having two eyes to be cast into hell fire.'"

Pleased with this last quote, Lazarus' head sank forward on his chest and he was soon sound asleep, snorting and gasping as he snored. Charlie decided to let him sleep it off where he lay, and headed over to the police department, which was just around the corner. He needed a place to think.

*****

44

Chapter Eight

Charlie had not been back at the police headquarters more than fifteen minutes when the door to the police department opened and Sankie Fenton entered.

"There's Gypsies in Ada!" he hollered. Ada was a small town about twelve miles from Shannon.

Charlie had been sitting back with his feet propped on his desk, ruminating. At the mention of Gypsies his feet came crashing down. He took in Sankie's knee-length pants, crew neck shirt, loud plaid vest, and newsboy cap. It was Sankie's town crier attire.

"Headed this way?" Charlie asked. The news was akin to a three-alarm fire. Every now and again the Travelers would pass through, driving big Cadillac touring cars. The cars would park on Main Street and the women, dressed in voluminous, brightly colored garb full of specially sewn-in pockets, would alight and disperse into various stores.

The hapless store owners were always outnumbered and easy victims to the plundering that followed. Mitchell Tanner, owner of the primary dry goods and women's apparel store on Main Street, could track one or two such customers, but half a dozen voracious Gypsy women, flitting about his store, could rob him blind. It was like a human shell game and he was no match for it.

Other scams the Travelers perpetrated on the unsuspecting locals included painting metal roofs with paint so thinned down it washed off after a heavy rain, and blacktopping driveways with worthless sealant that didn't last. Farm animals were up for grabs, too, particularly chickens and small pigs, as the marauders swept through the countryside.

"Maybe," Sankie said.

"You sure about this, Sankie?"

Sankie nodded. "Horace Amstutz just come from Ada. He said their Cadillacs was a pullin' into town as he was leavin'."

Forewarned was forearmed, Charlie thought. "Sankie, I need you to do somethin' for me. Pass up one side of Main Street and down the other and stop in all the stores and tell them what you just told me. Quietly, though. Don't shout it out that Gypsies are coming, got it? Pull the store owners aside and tell them, quiet like. Can you do that without raising a ruckus?"

Sankie nodded, excited. He was working for the police, and his chest swelled with pride. "I'll do it, Charlie," he said. "I'll do just what you asked." Sankie hurried out on his mission, full of importance.

*****

In the late 1890's, years called Shannon's Gay 90's, oil was discovered in the surrounding area, and an oil boom followed which brought in a new era of prosperity and growth. Farmers were approached constantly to allow drilling rights on their land. Some, such as Asa Simmons, Charlie's father, had gushers struck on their farmland.

One of the most productive oil wells in Shannon's history was located on old Asa's farm, making Asa a very wealthy man. Money from oil was the basis for Asa's ability to buy a farm for each of his sons, with the exception of his youngest son, Cliff. Cliff lacked the robust health his older brothers enjoyed that was needed to run a farm, so his father bought him a garage in Shannon, instead.

Charlie reckoned he had better check in with Cliff, and he headed down the street to the adjoining block where Cliff's garage was located. He found his younger brother in his office, hunched over a Chevrolet manual.

"Hey, Brother," Charlie said.

Startled, Cliff looked up, then smiled. "Charlie," he replied. "Things are a little slow in the garage right now …" He was on the verge of apologizing for not having any work for Charlie, but Charlie cut him off.

"No need, Cliff," he assured him. "Chief Gaite left me in charge while he's in Detroit and I've been busy with these barn fires."

"Ahhh…" Cliff said, nodding.

Charlie was protective of his little brother. Cliff, the youngest of Asa Simmons' seven kids, had also been the runt of the litter. His health had been delicate as a boy, and he had never been physically strong like his five older brothers. Even now he looked frail, his complexion anemic, veins visible on his forehead and temple under his slicked-down, sandy-colored thin hair. His pale blue eyes always seemed a bit rheumy to Charlie, and his back had a perpetual stoop to it.

Charlie flashed on the time when, in the one-room country school house where all the Simmons had gone to school, just down the road from Asa's farm, the school master had taken a cane to Cliff one day for some minor offense, almost crippling the boy. The school master, a Mr. Reese, had come from Tiffin, Ohio, and was a stranger to the Shannon community. As it turned out, he was also a bully.

The following day Cliff's older brothers, Horace, John, Orton, Jesse, and Charlie had shown up at the school house and set on the bully, forcing him to take refuge under his teacher's desk, which was much like a table, open on all sides. Every time he tried to crawl out from under the desk one of the Simmons boys would kick the hell out of him. After several rounds of this the Simmons brothers had gone home, leaving the school master with a broken arm and two broken ribs.

A few days later, with his ribs taped and his broken arm in a cast and sling, the school master drove his horse and buggy by Asa's farm and when Asa appeared he threatened, "I'm heading to town to press formal charges for what your boys did to me, Simmons."

Asa spat. "I'll go with you, Reese," he replied, "and report what you done to my youngest boy's back."

Reese giddapped his horse, and that was the last anyone ever saw of the school master in Shannon. You just didn't mess with the Simmons boys.

"Sankie Fenton says Horace Amstutz saw Gypsies flooding into Ada, Cliff," Charlie said.

Cliff took the news calmly. "Well, we know how to handle that," was all he said.

Charlie nodded. He knew the drill. Cliff and the men who worked in his garage would line up shoulder-to-shoulder in front of the entrance to the shop, large wrenches in their hands, telling the Travelers to stay out. It worked every time. There was something convincing about a small army of burly guys holding wrenches like they meant business.

*****

Chapter Nine

"Heard any more about whether the Gypsies are heading toward town, Charlie?"

Rolland had dropped by the police department during lunch on Thursday to chat with Uncle Charlie. He reached out to pet Lion, Charlie's cat, and Lion swiped his hand with a paw full of claws leaving three streaks turning red across the back of Rolland's hand. He yanked his hand back.

"Dang, Lion!"

Charlie grinned. Lion was his companion cat. Charlie walked Lion to the police station each morning on a leash, where he spent the day keeping Charlie company and entertaining the town folk who happened by. Lion was an enormous tan cat with a fringe of hair around his neck; hence, the name, Lion. He got on fine with everybody but Rolland.

"No, I haven't, Rolland. I'm thinking they went in the other direction, towards Tiffin. In any case, it's one less thing to worry about, what with these barn fires unsolved."

"Any idea who might have burnt them barns?"

Charlie was a strong believer in playing his cards close to this chest, even with Rolland. "Nothing concrete, Rolland. I wondered if the Gypsies might have had anything to do with it. And Lottsie Bassinger said he'd seen a suspicious guy from out of town hanging around, so there are several possibilities."

Rolland's eyes widened. "You really think Gypsies done it, Charlie?"

"Well now, Rolland, I can't ..."

Charlie was interrupted by Hiram Mohler stepping into his office. Hiram cleared his throat, shifting from one foot to the other. He wore his brown hair plastered to this head with some kind of pomade that smelled like horse liniment. He hadn't shaved for several days, judging by the dark stubble on his weathered face.

Charlie looked up at Hiram. "What can I do for you, Hiram?"

Hiram held an old battered fedora in his left hand, which he continuously turned round and round, pressing the brim with his right fingers as he did so. He cleared his throat again, and then spoke in his rasping voice.

"My Katie's missing," he said. Katie was his wife of twenty-five years. They had one daughter, now a widow with a young girl. The daughter and granddaughter sometimes lived with Hiram and Katie.

"What do you mean Katie's missing? Missing from where?" Charlie asked.

Mohler gave a helpless gesture with his hands. When he spoke again it sounded like he was close to tears.

"Katie's not at the farm," he said.

"Since when? When's the last time you saw her, Hiram?"

"Yestiddy morning, after milking," he said. "We finished turning the cows out and I told her I was a headin' over to my other farm to check on the grain in the storage bin. Moisture content's been a bit high."

"How long were you gone?"

"No more n' a couple hours. I was home in time for dinner, but she weren't there. Didn't have dinner on the table neither." He said this last as an accusation, as though Katie had committed an unpardonable sin against him.

"Could she have gone to visit someone, Hiram?"

Hiram was shaking his head.

"Doesn't she have any kin that live close by? Could she have gone to see any friends and not told you?"

Hiram continued to shake his head.

"What about your daughter, or granddaughter? Either of them know anything?"

Hiram was getting impatient with Charlie's questions. "Katie's gone, dammit! My Katie's gone, you hear?" And with that he stormed out of the police station, leaving the door wide open.

A stunned silence followed Hiram's departure. Charlie finally spoke.

"Well, hell," he said. Rolland waited, and waited. Silence. "That's it? A man comes in and says his wife's disappeared and 'well, hell' is it?"

Charlie swiveled around to face Rolland. "Look, Rolland," he began. "What I'm about to tell you goes no further than right here, between us, OK?"

Rolland was taken aback by Charlie's words; his curiosity piqued. He nodded. "Yeah, sure, Charlie."

Charlie paused. "I've known Hiram Mohler for nigh on twenty-six years. He's a nasty piece of work, Rolland, and has always treated Katie like his dog. For him to come in here acting all concerned and broke up just doesn't ring true to me. I hope I'm wrong, but damn!"

"What are you gonna do, Charlie?" Rolland wanted to know.

Charlie pursed his lips a moment, considering. "I guess I'll go out to his farm and talk to Evelyn, their daughter. See what she has to say about her mom gone missin'." He stood and got ready to leave. Rolland got out the door ahead of him and, as Charlie was making sure the door was secure, called after him, "Remember, Rolland: mum's the word."

*****

The trip to Mohler's farm proved fruitless. There was no sign, anywhere, of the Mohler daughter or granddaughter. The farm had a desolate air about it, and something even more foreboding Charlie could not identify. The place just gave him the creeps. He decided there wasn't anything for him to learn there, since no one was home, and headed back to his office.

*****

Chapter Ten

Life in Shannon had fallen back into the routine normalcy of small-town quiet. Aside from loud banter coming from the Eight Ball bar next door to Shalley's five-and-dime late Thursday afternoon Charlie was almost bored acting as the town's law enforcement officer.

He made himself visible all up and down Main Street, visiting with folks sitting on the benches along the sidewalks and checking the half dozen places where men loafed in Shannon. He stopped in the two pool rooms in town and spent time listening to the gossip that gets passed around in those two venues, had an afternoon coffee and piece of pie in The Pine, and passed an hour in Cliff's office at the garage, which was a favorite day-time haunt with some of the local farmers when they had a vehicle in for repair.

Charlie saved his favorite stop for last: JD's barber shop, at the corner of Main and Elm Streets. This particular barber shop was an institution in Shannon, having occupied the same place for over a hundred years. The names of the establishment had changed over time, but no matter whose name graced the sign over the door it was still one of the best hangouts in Shannon. If you wanted to get the low down on what was happening in town, JD's barber shop was the place to go.

Charlie paused next to the pole with a helix of red, white, and blue stripes that was the traditional sign for a barber shop. Back in the day, barber shops had performed basic healing practices, such as bloodletting (which often included using leeches). In Rome, barber surgeons at one time also pulled teeth, performed cupping, carried out minor surgeries, and administered enemas. Charlie reflected it was a good thing barbers had gotten out of the enema practice.

JD's was in the basement of the Dreshler business building; an insurance company took up the first and second floors. He descended the cement steps that led from the sidewalk to the barber shop's entrance. The opening of the door jingled a strip of chimes, designed to announce a customer. JD was finishing off a shave with a straight razor. He paused with the blade in mid-air.

"Charlie," he said, and resumed his craft.

"Afternoon, JD," Charlie replied. The scents of brilliantine, shaving oil, hair tonic, and pomade, mixed with tobacco smoke, all soothing scents, flavored the air. Charlie and hordes of Shannon men had been coming to this barbershop for decades, getting haircuts, shaves, and a dose of Shannon gossip in an atmosphere unique to JD's. There were other barbershops in town, but only one JD's.

The barber shop was a sanctuary, with its old wooden bench along the wall that fronted Main Street, coat rack in the corner, and an assortment of wooden chairs with worn leather seats placed along the wall that faced Elm Street. A table in the far corner was piled high with tattered magazines, back issues of the Shannon News, the local newspaper, and a well-worn King James Bible. Several Burma Shave posters graced the walls, as well as a framed picture of the American flag.

The wall opposite where the chairs were placed was covered in a large mirror with three sections. Two barber chairs sat in the available floor space in between, and the shelves in front of the mirrors were cluttered with razors, scissors, hand mirrors, boar's-hair brushes, and assorted hair products. A short, wooden, glass-topped display case, upon which sat an ancient ornate brass cash register with a 'National' logo on its front drawer, divided JD's workspace from the entrance. An assemblage of hair creams, plastic combs, brushes, Zippo cigarette lighters, and baseball cards arranged in the glass case had been collecting dust for years.

Coonie Denner, a real tightwad who owned a small grocery on Cherry Street, was complaining about one of the local churches spending money to fix up Jo Dale's falling down house. Charlie's wife, Faerie, used to shop at Denner's Grocery until she saw him wait on a family in the store one day.

Almost everything Coonie sold in his grocery was sold in bulk: flour, sugar, coffee, nuts. She watched him weigh out a pound of crackers on his scales for Moot Small's wife and kids, and she actually saw Coonie break the last cracker in two, placing half on the scale and the other half back in the cracker jar. Her thinking was you could not trust anybody that cheap, so she never shopped there again.

"You ask me, the deacons ought to spend the money on somethin' that'll help somebody who deserves it. They act like they got money to burn."

"Naked, and ye clothed me; I was sick, and ye visited me; I was in prison, and ye came unto me."

"And don't you go quoting scripture to me, Fred Birknauer," Coonie shot back. "The Lord helps those who help themselves."

"Blasphemy!" Fred muttered.

"What do you think, Charlie?" Foxy Worthington, one of the shop's patrons called out. All heads turned to where Charlie stood, leaning against the counter.

Charlie thought a moment, weighing his words. "Jo Dale's been a part of this community all his life," he said. "He's one of our neighbors. You help a neighbor in need."

Everyone nodded their agreement. Everyone except tightfisted Denner, who clamped his pipe stem between his teeth and looked straight ahead.

Just then Sankie Fenton hurried through the door slightly out of breath. "It's all over town that Katie Mohler's missin'," he said.

"Slow down, Sankie," JD said, finishing up his client with a spritz of hair tonic.

"What d'ya mean she's missin'?" Coonie Denner asked.

Charlie stepped forward. "All over town how, Sankie?" he asked. "Where did you hear about Katie Mohler?"

"It's her husband, Hiram, that's telling it," Sankie replied. He's drunk, over at the Eight Ball, crying in his beer about his wife disappearin'. They say he's been at it all day."

There was a stunned silence in the barber shop. Shannon was a small, close-knit community which included the town residents and those living on the surrounding farms. Life was simple; it ebbed and flowed. People did not just disappear in Shannon.

Turley Rupright said what everyone else was thinking. "Two barns burned in the space of a week and now a man's wife turns up missing. Nothing this big has happened in Shannon since Dillinger and his gang robbed the bank back in '33."

"Whoooee!" Foxy Worthington exclaimed. "That was somethin', the day they came to town! Remember that, Charlie?"

Indeed, Charlie remembered that day vividly. He had been a kid back then and was helping Aunt Ethel run the grill at The Pine restaurant when the robbery went down. Just before noon on August 14th he had heard what sounded like shots being fired outside.

Joe Birknauer had run into The Pine shouting, "The bank's being robbed!" but his reputation as a liar sent Charlie out the front door to see for himself. When several bullets whizzed by his head, he was convinced Joe was, for once, telling the truth, and he ducked back inside.

The Shannon Citizen's National Bank was just two short blocks up and across Main Street from The Pine. Two members of the gang had stood out in front of the bank, spraying bullets up and down Main Street and, also, down Church Street, that ran alongside the bank, from a sub-machine gun and two revolvers. Windows in buildings across from the bank and up and down Main Street were shattered by the random shooting, designed to keep Shannon's population off the streets.

In particular, Charlie remembered Kenny Shine, a salesman from Lima who had spent the morning in Shannon calling on clients and was waiting for the bus to take him home. The bus stop was outside The Pine restaurant and Kenny had time to kill so he had walked uptown. He got caught on the corner opposite and diagonal from the bank, in front of the Presbyterian Church, with only a waist-high drinking fountain and a narrow boulevard light post for cover.

After the robbery ordeal was over Kenny had hurried back to the restaurant, where he told Charlie how he had escaped getting shot by the Dillinger gang.

"I jumped behind the lamp post and I d-d-d-drawed in my breath, and I d-d-d-drawed in my breath, 'til I thought the top of my head would shoot out over the top of the lamp post!"

Turley spoke up. "I was living in the apartments above the bakery, at the time," he said. "When I heard the gun fire, I ran down to the sidewalk to see what was goin' on, and one of the gangsters snapped off a couple a' rounds at me. It was quicker to jump behind one of the cars parked on the street than to try and get back to the apartment, so that's just what I did. I lay down flat on the pavement and stayed there until the gang left town."

Charlie never forgot that day, amazed that no one in Shannon had been wounded or killed in the brazen robbery which only netted the Dillinger gang twenty-five hundred bucks. In the end, the gang was killed off one by one, John Dillinger himself shot outside a theater in Chicago when the Lady in Red, a Romanian immigrant, gave him up to the Feds in return for not being deported for amoral behavior.

"You hear anything more about the Gypsies, if they're heading this way, Charlie?" JD asked, changing the subject.

"No, I have not," he answered. "But since it's come up, any of you ever hear of Gypsies startin' fires or burnin' down barns?" he asked the men sitting around the barber shop.

They all thought a bit, looking around at each other, squirming in their seats. One by one, they finally admitted that no, they had not heard of Gypsies starting fires … just stealin' chickens and anything not nailed down.

That confirmed Charlie's feelings on the subject, too. He tried a different tack. "Anybody know this Zack Cooper from Rawson?"

"Yeah, I know him, Charlie," Turley Rupright said.

All heads turned to Turley, then back to Charlie.

Charlie scratched his right cheek. "What d'ya know, Turley?"

"Aw, he's alright, I guess. Bit of a loner with a sour outlook on life, but more bark than bite. He's married to my wife's cousin. Why?"

"You think he had anything to do with the Gratz brothers' barns burnin'?"

All heads were back on Turley, awaiting his answer. You could have heard a pin drop.

Turley was momentarily taken aback. "Lord, no!" he finally said. "You want to know who I think's behind them barns a burnin' you should ask Clyde Gratz who he and Tom caught stealin' planks from their rail fences."

The audience let out a collective gasp. Now this was news.

*****

Chapter Eleven

"You didn't think to mention this to me earlier, Clyde?" Charlie asked. It was Friday morning and he'd stopped by Clyde Gratz' farm to ask about the fence rail situation. He was more than a little frustrated that neither Clyde nor Tom Gratz had told him about their run-in with old Hiram Mohler a month or so back.

He had caught Clyde as he was finishing up work on his tractor. His bib overalls were streaked with grease and mud.

Clyde ducked his head, embarrassed. "Well, gee, Charlie," he fumbled, "I didn't think much of it at the time. Ol' Hiram always has a bee in his bonnet about somethin'…" Clyde was trying to light his pipe, but the grease on his hands made that difficult as the pipe kept slipping. He finally pulled his grease rag from his rear pocket and wiped his hands clean.

"But he was *stealing* from you boys, Clyde, and you caught him at it."

Charlie made Clyde go over the incident again to be sure he had it straight.

"Me and Tom was checkin' the fence line between our land and Hiram's," he began. "We keep the briars and natural growth along that strip of land … encourages the pheasant population … and wanted to check that the fence rails were still in place, and we saw Hiram down there with a wagon a loadin' up rails he'd taken off our fence."

"Did he see you?" Charlie asked.

"Well, hell yes," Clyde said. "Tom shouted at him to quit stealing our fence."

"What did Hiram do when Tom said that?"

Clyde colored in anger at the memory. "He shook his fist at us, and swore, and said we'd live to regret it."

"Live to regret what, Clyde?"

"Live to regret that we didn't just let him carry on a stealin' our fence, I guess."

'Sounds like Hiram,' Charlie thought. "Then what'd he do?"

"He threw the rail he had in his hands onto his wagon, giddapped his horse, and hauled off our fence rails."

"Why was he using a horse and not a tractor?" Charlie wanted to know.

"The land's a little wet there and pretty overgrown. A tractor might get bogged down."

"On his side of the fence or yours?"

"Both," Clyde said.

Charlie called in on Tom Gratz directly after speaking with his brother, Clyde, to get his version of the story. Tom's rendition was the same as Clyde's, except he remembered that Hiram said he'd 'be back', in addition to the part about living to regret it.

"Charlie, it's Pete Gaite. How goes things in Shannon?"

"Oh, hey, Pete. Things are fine here. How's your sister?"

"She's fine, thanks. Say, Charlie, the wife called me last night and told me it's all over town that Katie Mohler's gone missin'. Is that the truth?"

"According to Hiram, yes," Charlie, replied.

"Well, cripes, Charlie," Pete said, "do you need me to come home?"

"Naw, Pete," he replied. "Everything's under control. You just take care of your sister, like you said. If I need anything, I'll be sure and let you know."

*****

Chapter Twelve

Harvest Festival in Shannon was an anticipated annual event, coming on the heels of the corn harvest in the fall. The whole town pitched in, along with the local churches, to celebrate and give thanks for a plentiful harvest.

Main Street was closed off for several blocks from Jefferson Street to College Avenue, and a large banner spanned the street at each end, proclaiming a two-day jubilee. Bales of straw were arranged up and down the street and topped with pumpkins, squash, shocks of corn, pots of chrysanthemums, and colorful gourds by way of decoration. Red, white, and blue bunting was draped around the lamp posts, and a viewing stand was erected on the lawn of the Presbyterian Church.

The three main churches in town, First Mennonite, First United Methodist, and Presbyterian, opened their fellowship halls and kitchens for community-wide meals cooked by Shannon's wives, mothers, and daughters as fund raisers for local causes. There were vast displays of jams, jellies, nut butters, relishes, pickled vegetables, candied fruits, and chow-chow relish in a range of hotness. Judges were brought in from neighboring farm communities to impartially choose the best of each category.

Tables laden with pies, cakes, breads, and cookies were set up in the fellowship halls. These delicacies were to be judged, as well, and the specimens then sold off in a bake auction. Recipes of the winning entries also had a price put on them. Competition was fierce but civility was maintained, even if superficially. Hell hath no fury like a woman scorned, and a woman in competition with her baked goods was especially flammable.

Activities for the men in the community included pole throwing, a tractor pull, livestock judging, hog calling, bull whip cracking, and horseshoes. Shannon's only remaining livery barn, located behind the main business section of town along Main Street, had been turned into an exhibition area for rabbits, chickens, goats, and sheep, and hog and cattle pens had been erected on the barn's west side that was the town's main parking lot.

A pony ride around a ring afforded entertainment for kids, as well as sack races, three-leg races, a ring toss, apple bobbing, and a petting zoo. Kid's art, culled from the local schools, was on display, grouped according to age, and would be judged with small cash prizes awarded.

There was something for everybody at the celebration, which ran on Friday and Saturday, with everyone going to their respective church on Sunday morning to give thanks to the Lord for another year of blessing with a pleasant look forward to Thanksgiving and then the sacred holiday of Christmas.

The festival was opened, officially, by Mayor Alan Baker from the viewing stand at ten o'clock on Friday morning. Alan was in his third term as mayor. Shannon born-and-raised, he owned and operated the dry-cleaning business at Main and Cherry streets. His wife taught American History at Shannon High and helped out at their cleaning business on Saturdays and after school. They were just ordinary citizens who had earned the community's trust through their service and honesty.

He gave a short speech praising all the hard effort and community spirit that went into making the festival a success, bragged on the quality of life Shannon afforded and the goodness of the citizens he was fortunate to represent, wished luck to those in the various competitions, and encouraged everyone to have a grand time. Everyone applauded, politely.

The pastor from the Presbyterian Church spoke next, reminding all gathered that their blessings came from God, quoting several scriptures to make his point, and ended in a prayer of thanksgiving for the Lord's provision and protection. This was followed by a collective 'Amen.'

Mayor Baker then declared that the festival had begun. His announcement was followed by church bells ringing and the big whistle at the water plant sounding off. Handbills listing the day and time of the scheduled contests and events were passed out and then the crowd lined Main Street, waiting for the annual Harvest Festival parade to begin.

It was short and sweet, but a requisite of the festival. Mounted horses sporting fancy bridles and saddles, docile cows adorned with fall flowers herded down the street by teenagers, mostly, kids on bicycles, and brothers pulling little sisters in wagons, with some holding a puppy or cat. And last, but not least, the Shannon High School marching band, such as it was, playing the high school's fight song and 'God Bless America.'

*****

Chapter Thirteen

For weeks, the god-fearing citizens of Shannon had been plagued by the appearance of a ghost in the local Maple Grove Cemetery. The ghost would rise out of the ground, visible in the moonlight, and then slowly disappear back into the earth. The apparition did this in several locations in the cemetery, and then would appear no more. Residents from Shannon would congregate at the bridge to watch the specter's appearance, going no closer for fear of being damned or spiritually doomed.

On the opening night of the Harvest Festival, Friday, just after darkness had fallen, the ghost rose again. The night made a soft inky-black background for the silver highlights cast down by the full moon. The customary crowd of town's people gathered at the bridge, afraid to go any further.

Suddenly, a college student stepped forward, boldly brandishing a pistol.

"This has been going on long enough," he declared. "It's about time somebody found out what this ghost business is all about." He started toward the cemetery's double wrought-iron gates with determination in his step.

"Ohhhh! Bring that boy back! He'll surely be lost!" several of the women standing on the bridge cried out, terrified for his immortal soul.

When he was about twenty yards inside the cemetery gates the young man fired several shots in the air and yelled, "Who's out there?"

A voice hollered back, "Don't shoot, for cripes sake! It's Med Murphy!"

"Come out with your hands up!" the college boy ordered.

Med came shuffling out, hands up and eyes wide. "Don't shoot," he said, again. "It was just a joke."

The crowd that was gathered at the bridge started to boo when they saw who the ghost was.

"Shame on you Med Murphy!" one woman yelled. "Your poor mother!"

"You oughtta get a good hiding," another woman scolded.

The crowd grumbled their agreement. They were getting a bit restless and the mood had changed from one of fear to one of retribution. The college kid was afraid things might get out of hand and the crowd would descend on Med, so he shoved Med in the direction of town and announced he was running the culprit in to the police station.

"No need, Son," a voice said.

The crowd parted and Charlie Simmons strode forward.

"Med Murphy," Charlie intoned, "I'm arresting you on grounds of terrifying the public and creating a near-riot." He pulled a pair of handcuffs off his belt and secured Med's wrists and started to lead him away. He turned back. "The rest of you go on home. No harm's been done and the show's over." Charlie took ahold of Med's arm and pulled him along, heading up town towards the jail. He asked the college kid to come along, too, in case he had questions for him.

At the police station, when he was sure no one else was about and with the college kid sequestered in another room, Charlie pitched into Med.

"What the hell you thinking, Med Murphy, scaring your neighbors like that with some stupid prank?"

Med hung his head. "It was George McComb who put me up to it," he mumbled. "Me and Dave Hightower."

Charlie's eyebrows raised. "George McComb, you say? The undertaker?" He was incredulous.

Med looked Charlie in the eye and nodded.

"Now see here, Med," Charlie chided, "what's behind all this? Explain it to me, Son."

So, Med began. "George's the undertaker," he said, "but he also sells sewing machines and window blinds as a side business."

"Yes, yes, I know," Charlie said, impatiently.

"Well, he had this idea how to play a prank on the town people with one of his window blinds and approached me an' Dave to do it for him." He paused. "George painted a skeleton on one of his black window blinds with some phosphoric paint that showed up real good in the moonlight. He mounted the blind on a narrow board with pins at each end that could fasten the blind to the ground. He'd already taken off the ratchet mechanism.

"Me and Dave would sneak into the cemetery when the moon was bright and hide in the shadows. We'd tromp on the board to lodge the pins in the ground and throw a stone with a string attached to it over a low tree limb. The other end of the string was tied to a loop on the top of the blind. Then we'd slowly pull on the string and the blind would unroll with the skeleton glowing in the moonlight. It looked like the skeleton was coming up out of the ground. We'd raise and lower it a couple times, real slow, then move the blind to another part of the cemetery and do it all over again."

Charlie couldn't help it; his face lit up with a huge grin. "Ingenious!" Med heard him say. He summoned the college kid to join them and, when the kid sat down, Charlie questioned him.

"How'd you get involved in all this?" he asked. "What's your name, by the way?"

"Howard," the college boy stammered. "Howard Clay."

"Pleased to meet you, Howard," Charlie said. "Now, tell me how you came to be at the bridge tonight with a pistol full of blanks."

"Some guy stopped me when I was coming out of my dorm several nights ago and told me what was really going on with the ghost in the cemetery," Howard said. "I thought he was pulling my leg, but he assured me that what he said was the truth. He identified himself as the town undertaker, so I believed him. Then he said he wanted me to play the hero with the gun and all. He said the prank had gone on long enough and the town people were getting too worried, especially the women." He shrugged. "I agreed to do what he said for ten bucks."

"Why that lousy, double-crossing …" Med was halfway out of his seat, but Charlie waved him back.

He looked at Med. "You said Dave Hightower was in on this with you?"

Med nodded.

"What happened to him? Where is he?"

"He ran off when the shots were fired," Med said.

"Any idea where he could have gone?" Charlie asked.

"If I had to guess I'd say he lit out for his sister's place on the Zurflugh Road, west of town."

Charlie grinned. "OK, Med, this is what I want you to do …"

*****

"Hi, Sophie. Is Dave there?"

"Who's this?"

"It's Med Murphy, Sophie. I need to speak with Dave if he's there." There was a brief pause.

"Med?" Dave had come on the line.

"Yeh, it's me, ole buddy. Listen, the law's looking for you, so you gotta lay low for a while. I'm out on bail, but that Charlie Simmons is fired up and wants you brought in for questioning."

Dave turned white at Med's news. "Uh, OK, Med. Thanks for the warning," he said.

For the next week, every time Dave Hightower heard an automobile on the country road that ran past his sister's, house he thought they were coming for him and ran out and dove in his sister's raspberry patch to hide. At the end of the week he was a miserable mass of scratches.

Med called Dave, again, after a week had passed. "Dave, it's
Med. It's OK to come out of hiding. The police decided to let
the whole thing pass as a prank, so you don't have to hide
anymore."

"You don't know how glad I am to hear that," Dave sighed.
He told Med about hiding in the berry patch.

"Well, it's all over with, now," he assured Dave. 'And that's
what you get for runnin' off and leavin' me holding the bag,'
Med added, to himself, with a satisfied smirk.

*****

Chapter Fourteen

The highlight of the festival for Shannon's teenagers came on Saturday night with the hayride. A buck wagon filled with fragrant hay, pulled by a tractor, left the parking lot near the livery barn, winding its way through the countryside around town while its passengers sipped hot chocolate from thermoses, telling ghost stories, singing songs, and just having a good time. Usually included on the itinerary was traversing or stopping near a cemetery. The high schoolers, in an unspoken ritual, would somehow pair off during the ride, the pairings implying interest, possibility, and ownership.

Snuggled down in the warmth of the hay, the teens would shyly enact age-old social rites which, the participants hoped, would carry forth once the magic time of festival had passed. The hayride was recognized as the impetus for more than a few couples tying the proverbial knot. In short, for the older teenagers it was a mating ritual.

The hayride arrived back at the old barn around eleven o'clock, dispersing its passengers. Lenny Kuhn and Marilyn Lehman had snuck into the livery barn to find a soft spot in the straw to further explore the feelings they had for one another. Their hormones were raging.

"Oh, Len," Marilyn moaned. She was pretty much in a state of undress, and Len wasn't far behind.

"Yeh, Baby," he cooed. The bulge in his pants made it difficult to maneuver them off.

"Oh, hurry!" she gasped. Somewhere, some movie she had seen had left an imprint of a tryst and she was following the script. She really had no idea what was coming next and boy, was she in for a surprise!

Len fumbled with his belt buckle, finally managing to get it loose. Marilyn writhed in the straw beneath him, incensing him even more. She reached over her head in a state of ecstasy, like she'd seen in the movies, and felt a hand.

She looked at Len; both his hands were working to undo his jeans. She groped further, feeling the cold, stiff fingers.

"Oh my God!" she screamed.

Len was frustrated. "I'm trying, Marilyn," he told her. "Just give me a sec, OK?"

Marilyn bolted into a sitting position, a look of terror on her face.

"Len," she said, "it's cold and hard."

He grinned sheepishly. "It's hard, alright, Baby, but it sure ain't cold. I'm on fire!"

Marilyn rolled away from where she had been laying, pulling on her clothes, fumbling to fasten them. She was almost hysterical.

"Marilyn," he said, "where you goin', Baby? I thought we had somethin'…"

"There's a body in the straw, Len," she croaked. She was visibly shivering. "A dead body."

*****

Chapter Fifteen

"There's no doubt about what killed him," Doc Steiner, Shannon's medical examiner and sole doctor, said after a quick look at the lifeless body of Otto Hilty where he lay, partially covered by straw bedding in the livery barn. He shone his flashlight on the dead man's face.

Involuntarily, Charlie recoiled in horror at the rusty bail hook that had been imbedded in Otto's right eye, killing him with the brain trauma it inflicted. A cascading wash of drying blood under his destroyed eye colored an otherwise pallid visage.

"Good God!" he exclaimed. Charlie had seen gore in his days, but this was over the top. He felt like he had entered the Twilight Zone.

"I'd estimate the time of death sometime between eight and ten o'clock this evening," Doc said. "He died almost instantly. I'd say whoever did this didn't plan it; use of the bail hook suggests more a spur of the moment act and the bail hook was the first thing at hand." He sighed. "Send Otto onto the morgue at the hospital, Charlie. I'll do a preliminary exam and put in a call to the coroner to set up an autopsy."

Charlie put in a request to transfer the body to the hospital. Doc left to prepare for the promised examination of Otto's corpse. Charlie went to the door of the livery barn and looked out on the crowd that had gathered. The thought occurred to him that the murderer was likely somewhere nearby, and his gaze travelled thoughtfully over the faces before him. These folks were his friends and neighbors, people he had grown up with, but one of them had the mark of Cain stamped on his soul this night.

He signaled Rolland Simmons and Med Murphy out of the crowd and motioned for them to come forward. He pulled the two young men into the barn to speak to them.

"Rolland and Med," he began, "by the powers invested in me as acting police chief of this town I'm deputizing the two of you tonight. I want you to spend the night in this livery barn to make sure no one sneaks in and messes with the crime scene."

"What crime scene?" Med asked.

Charlie looked at him in surprise. "Where you been tonight, Med?" he asked.

Med looked embarrassed. "I been playing cards at the Eight Ball," he confessed.

"The Eight Ball's a hangout for riffraff, Med," Charlie said. "Not the sort of place I would expect to find Med Murphy frequenting. Your dad know you go there?"

Med started shifting from one foot to the other. "I guess not, Charlie," he said. "It was only the second time," he defended. "An' I'm done with the place. Dad don't have to know." His eyes pleaded for leniency.

"Last night you got caught playing folks in Shannon for fools with your ghost routine, tonight you're hanging out with low life in the pool hall." He fixed a stern eye on Med. "This better be your last night there, Son."

Med winced at Charlie's words. He came from a good family; his father ran the local post office and was a deacon in his church, his mother a schoolteacher. If they knew what Med had been up to with the ghost scenario they would have been embarrassed, but his hanging out in the pool hall would have scandalized them.

"Is it true Otto was killed with a bail hook in his eye?" Rolland blurted.

Charlie eyed his nephew. "Who told you that, Rolland?"

Rolland gestured toward the congregation of town people gathered outside the barn. "It's no secret, Charlie," he explained. "Everybody out there knows about it. Is it true?"

Charlie nodded.

Med's eyes almost popped out of his head. "And you want us to spend the night in a barn where a man died?"

"Murdered," Rolland corrected. "Otto was murdered."

Charlie shot him a wry look that said 'thanks'.

"Jesus, Mary, and Joseph!" was all Med could say.

Rolland spoke up; his voice had taken on a tone of serious importance.

"Let me run home and tell Ethel what I'm doing, and I'll fetch a sleeping bag from Pap's house, too."

Charlie nodded. "You got a sleeping bag Med can use?"

Rolland nodded before slipping off for his dad's house, which was a two-minute walk from the barn.

Charlie turned back to Med. "You OK to stay here tonight with Rolland?"

"I-I guess so," he replied.

Charlie clapped him on the shoulder. "I appreciate your help Med. I'll call your dad and let him know you're assisting me with the investigation. He won't mind."

*****

Chapter Sixteen

Charlie had sent everyone home from the livery barn and by the time Rolland returned with the sleeping bags, a thermos of hot coffee and a half dozen of his Aunt Ethel's homemade rolls things had quieted down. The kerosene lantern Charlie had left cast long, eerie shadows around them.

"You ever seen anyone dead before?" Med asked Rolland, almost in a whisper.

Rolland nodded but said nothing.

"What was it like? Who was it?"

Med's morbid curiosity called up unwanted images in Rolland's mind.

"I was eleven years old and living with my grandma on Railroad Street," he began. "Old Mr. Hauenstein, who lived two doors down, was standing on the sidewalk outside the front of his house late one afternoon motioning people inside. 'Go on in, go on in,' he kept saying." Rolland took a swig of coffee.

"His wife was laying in the middle of the kitchen floor, burned to death. She'd thrown some kindling in the wood stove and her greasy apron caught fire … and there he was … out of his head, ushering folks in to look at his charred wife like it was the most natural thing in the world. I'll never forget that smell as long as I live," he added.

There was silence for a while, both young men lost in their thoughts. Med spoke first.

"Is it true what you said, Rolland, that Otto was killed by a bail hook?"

Rolland nodded. "Hooked him right through the eye, and into his brain."

Med shuddered. "Who'd do something like that?" he asked, himself as much as Rolland.

Eventually, the two young deputies drifted off to sleep. Rolland drew steady, deep breaths in an easy sleep, but Med's sleep thoughts were full of nightmarish images. Mutilated corpses, dismembered faces in hideous grimaces, and the sense of being chased made Med toss and turn fitfully. He cried out several times, and finally jolted awake. He had heard something in the barn, and it was not the animals caged there.

He nudged Rolland and, when he got no response, pinched him.

"What the …" Rolland began, still half asleep.

"Someone's in the barn," Med whispered. That woke Rolland, instantly.

"Where?" Rolland whispered back.

Med was straining to hear. "There!" he hissed. "Over by the watering trough."

Rolland groped for his flashlight and in doing so knocked over the thermos. The aluminum clanged on the cement floor.

Something skirmished toward the entrance. He found his torch, turned it on and focused it on the barn door. They felt, rather than saw, a furtive movement just beyond the flashlight's beam, then stillness. Not a sound.

They agreed it was best to stay where they were and not look for the intruder. The mental image of a bail hook protruding from Otto Hilty's eye convinced them this was the wisest course of action. The remainder of the night, however, they stayed awake, saying little, waiting for the sun to rise.

*****

"You're sure someone came to the barn last night?" Charlie asked.

Med and Rolland nodded.

"But you didn't see anyone?"

Med shook his head. "I heard whoever it was moving, and sensed, rather than saw 'im." Rolland nodded his agreement with what Med said.

A thorough search had been made of the barn's interior in the light of day, which included checking the animal cages and pens, but nothing useful was discovered. The pile of straw where the body had been discovered had been disturbed by the teenagers who had tried to make a love nest there, so there was no way of telling if there had been much of a struggle.

Charlie headed to the morgue to meet with Doc Steiner. Doc did not have much to add, other than whoever killed Otto Hilty had attacked him from behind and was a right-handed

89

person, due to the weapon used and the way it had been lodged in his skull.

"So what?" Charlie said, thinking aloud. "Some random stranger hiding in the livery barn just skewers Otto's head for no good reason? The chances of that are almost nil, since we don't have raving lunatics wandering around Shannon. No, it must have been someone he knew, but why turn his back on him?"

Doc had been listening to Charlie's progression of thought, and when he paused, asked, "What if Otto was meeting somebody in the barn last night?"

Charlie looked at that a moment and nodded his head. "Otto's waiting, looking toward the door for the person to arrive, but the guy's already in the barn. He's hiding, somewhere behind Otto. Otto has his back to the guy 'cause he's looking out, waiting. He doesn't know the other guy is there ahead of him . . ."

"And the murderer attacks Otto from behind, taking him by surprise," Doc finished.

"So, that scenario makes the attack sound planned, after all," Charlie said.

That sounded right to both men, and they nodded in agreement.

"The coroner's autopsy should be able to tell us if he was drugged or had been drinking prior to the assault. Also, it'll tell us when Otto ate last, … stomach contents may give us more information about where he'd been and when."

Charlie nodded. "I need to interview the hayride participants," Charlie said. "Maybe one of the kids saw somebody near the barn when the hayride got back or noticed something odd." He started for the door, stopped, and turned back to Doc. "Good work, Doc," he said, "get back to me with the coroner's findings," and left.

*****

Charlie got a list of the kids who were on the hayride and, one by one, tracked them down and interviewed them about who they may have seen in or near the livery barn the previous night. The only morsel of information he gleaned from the teens was that Mrs. Studler's tom cat, Hercules, had been serenading from atop a nearby wooden fence when the hayride returned to the barn and had run off when Kylie Mason pitched an ear of corn at him. Other than that, no one remembered seeing or hearing anything out of the ordinary.

*****

Chapter Seventeen

The townspeople were stunned by a murder in Shannon, particularly that of such a well-known resident. Otto Hilty had been born and raised in Shannon. Otto pretty much kept to himself and had become even more of a recluse since his mother, Janie Rose, had died four years ago. She had been the only close family he had, since Broman Hilty, his father, had never come home from WWII. The Hilty's in his lineage were all a bit peculiar; this was attributed to too much inter-marriage in the settlement in past generations.

Otto worked as a mail carrier in Shannon; he had been picking up and delivering mail for almost nine years. He was the only person with a perfect on-the-job attendance record in the entire Shannon post office. His dedication to his job was almost the butt of jokes in the rural community.

He was in his mid-thirties and lived alone in a small, wooden-frame house on the south end of Jackson Street. It was the house where he had grown up. He had never married which, in such a conservative community, raised eyebrows and fed the rumor mill. It seemed his only passion in life was the prize dahlias he grew in the postage-stamp size garden that encompassed his home.

From the middle of summer until frost Otto's dahlias drew onlookers from a radius of fifty miles to his modest home. Water lily dahlias, pom pom dahlias, cactus dahlias, ball dahlias, single and double petal specimens … all in an array of colors that delighted the visual sense. Otto's garden was a slice of heaven for the local bee population.

Area newspapers sent reporters out to interview Otto and photograph the amazing dahlias in their colored splendor, but Otto generally declined to talk to them. Various garden clubs begged to include his showy flowers on their annual garden walks, but he politely told them 'no.' He took to tending his lovelies in the evening and on into the dark of night to avoid being harassed while he trimmed, dead-headed, watered, fertilized, and mulched.

When Charlie pulled up in front of Otto's home the Sunday afternoon following his murder, he wondered what would become of the blooms that reigned over all the flower beds, insulating the plain white house from lackluster dreariness. He caught a movement at a side window in a neighboring house as someone let the lace curtain fall back into place.

He let himself in with the key he had taken from the pants Otto had been wearing the night before. Even in that short span of time, the house had a closed-up smell. Charlie called out "Anyone home?" It was an irrational reaction; he knew that Otto lived alone, and the house was empty. He didn't even have a cat.

Charlie wound his way, respectfully, through the dead man's home. He was surprised at the newness of the furnishings. 'Expensive taste,' he thought. Otto's kitchen confirmed this, as well: all-new appliances, first-quality built-in cabinets, and tray lighting over the prep area altered Charlie's misconception that Otto's home was that of a bachelor scraping by.

The theme of self-indulgence was carried out in the bedroom, as well. A large, mahogany bed with ormolu inlay, flanked on each side by matching nightstands, commanded Charlie's attention. It was an upscale bedroom suite, he knew. The console stereo and large collection of LP records represented a sizeable outlay of cash, as well. Charlie thumbed through the country western albums arranged alphabetically by artist. It wasn't that Otto's life had been one of luxury, but certainly far more comfortable than a postal carrier's salary would accommodate.

'Why murder Otto?' Charlie wondered. 'Was it the act of a crazed stranger? If that were the case,' Charlie reasoned, 'there would be nothing helpful in his house to point toward his killer.' Charlie sat in the rocking desk chair in front of Otto's immaculate mahogany desk. Mentally, he ticked off reasons people had for murdering another human being: Money. Anger. Jealousy. Revenge. Which would it be in Otto's case?

He began a systematic search of the desk. The drawers down the left-hand side yielded nothing of interest. They contained writing pads, assorted Hallmark greeting cards for a variety of occasions, pens, pencils, a stapler, and extension cords. Drawers on the desk's right side contained personal papers, a deed to the house, insurance policy, Otto's birth certificate, his record of baptism in the local Methodist church, and birthday and valentine cards from his mom, tied in a bundle, spanning his entire life up until four years ago when she had passed on.

The large, single drawer in the middle of the desk held Otto's bank book and a collection of paid bills, as well as a scotch tape dispenser, paper clips, and an address book that had never been written in. Nothing stood out, but Charlie pocketed the bank book. He glanced at the three framed photos on the desktop. One showed Otto with his mom, taken before she died, obviously, at the annual fishing derby held at Shannon's Buckeye Lake. He could just make out the year, 1951, on the banner in the background.

A second picture, taken professionally in the local Balmer studio, showed a young couple in their twenties, still in love and hopeful for their future together. Charlie recognized Broman and Janie Rose, Otto's parents. The third photograph was of an Otto in his early teens, grinning beside a shy-looking girl several years his junior. Charlie had no idea who the girl was, but Otto looked fairly normal. Not like the balding, slightly stooped eccentric he had become.

He let himself out the way he had come, making sure to lock up. Meredith Templeton, one of Otto's neighbors, stood by the fence between her house and Otto's. It seemed she had something to say to Charlie, so he obliged her by walking over to where she stood.

"'Afternoon, Meredith," he said, easily.

Meredith Templeton nodded curtly and sniffed by way of a reply.

"Somethin' I can do for you, Meredith?" he asked the old maid who was not a day younger than sixty.

"I need protecting, Charlie Simmons," she said.

"Protecting from what, Maa'm?"

"From the same person who killed Otto Hilty," she declared, dumbfounded that she had to explain it to Charlie.

Charlie gave his slow, easy smile. "And who would that be, then?" he asked.

"Whoever tried to break into his house in the wee hours of this morning," she replied.

Charlie's ears pricked up. "Someone was at Otto's, Meredith? What time was this?"

Meredith's face took on a supremely smug look. She had information Charlie wanted; now he would listen to her.

"Lemme see," she began, looking skyward. She glanced slyly down to see if he was waiting and was rewarded to see he hung on her every word. "I let Dumpling out for her tinkle at one o'clock," she said. A ratty-looking little dog with a cracked rhinestone dog collar yipped when Meredith said her name. "Hush, Dumpling," she said, shooing with her hand. "Whoever it was ran off when I switched on my porch light."

"How do you know it was that time?" he asked her.

She gaped at him, incredulously. "BECAUSE," she said, "I looked at the clock!" She bent down to pick Dumpling up in her arms. "Let's go, Precious," she cooed to the dog. "You believe Mama, don't you?"

Charlie watched her go and wondered if everyone who lived on this end of Jackson Street was nuts. His visit to Otto's house had given him vital information: he had not been killed randomly; whoever had murdered Otto Hilty knew him and, also, knew where he lived. And there was something in that house that the killer wanted, or did not want, discovered.

*****

Chapter Eighteen

Back in his office, Charlie looked through Otto Hilty's bank book. It was kept in a flawless hand, the dates and amounts entered legibly and neatly. He glanced down the columns of numbers, noting the repeating numbers deposited on a monthly basis. The largest amount, entered once a month, was undoubtedly Otto's salary from the US Postal Service.

There were other, smaller amounts that recurred, as well. The third of each month listed a deposit of fifty-five dollars and went back as far as the book would record, to 1952. Another amount for seventy dollars was posted to the account between the tenth and thirteenth of each month and had been deposited for the past year and a half. A third deposit in the amount of one hundred dollars, even, went into Otto's account on the twenty first of each month, going back to 1953.

'Regular as prune juice,' Charlie thought.

He wondered about the source of these monthly deposits. Did Charlie own stocks or bonds? Was he clipping coupons? Did he do odd jobs on the side? If so, why were the amounts always the same? An insurance policy that was paying out? Had his parents left him funds? These were all valid questions. He would need to go back to Charlie's house and look through his desk again.

The phone rang. It was Pete.

"Criminelly, Charlie, what the hell's goin' on down there?" he almost shouted.

"Oh, hey, Pete. Well, Otto Hilty was murdered last night in the livery barn and …"

"Heavenly cripes! The wife called me this morning and told me!"

Charlie wished Pete's wife would stop doing that. He was tired of Pete hyperventilating over the telephone at him.

"I really think I should come home, but my sister's got to go in for a procedure so I'm stuck here in Detroit for another week, at least. Do you think you should call in some law enforcement assistance from Lima?"

"Naw, Pete," Charlie assured him. "I'm close to apprehending the person who killed Otto. Don't you worry. Gotta go, Pete," he said, and rang off. He wondered if he could legally cancel Mrs. Gaite's phone service for a week or so.

*****

"Did you hear the latest about Katie Mohler?" Rolland asked Charlie when he stopped by his office on his way to The Pine to work the breakfast shift early Monday morning. Lion was cleaning himself on Charlie's desk, paying particular attention to his nether regions. He paused, mid-lick, tongue half-way out of his mouth, to eyeball Rolland. Rolland kept his distance.

Charlie looked up from Otto's bank book. "What's that?" he asked.

"Old Man Mohler is offering five hundred bucks for information about his wife's disappearance or where she is," Rolland told him.

100

Charlie digested this new information. "How'd you hear about this?"

"It's all over town, Uncle Charlie," Rolland replied. "Everybody's talkin' about it."

"Hmmmm," was all Charlie had to say.

*****

Chapter Nineteen

Monday morning, just after nine o'clock, Charlie went back to the Hilty house hoping to find more information about the source of the monthly deposits to Otto's bank account. He sat in the desk chair, as before, and methodically searched the desk again. He found the last will and testament of Janie Rose Hilty, in which she left all her worldly possessions to her 'only child, Otto.'

A short list following this declaration named the house on Jackson Street, her china, and the contents of the home. No mention was made of any insurance policy or annuity. Nothing to explain the regular deposits. On the other hand, the monthly additions to Otto's bank account, over and above his paycheck, explained the standard of living on display in his home.

Charlie sat back in the rocking desk chair, lightly tapping the arms of the chair with his fingers. His gaze swept over the surface of the desktop, stopped, and swept back. A thin rectangle of glossy mahogany shone from where it was outlined by the dust that had accumulated on the desk's top. Charlie started when he realized what the glossy area was. It was where the framed picture of young Otto and the timid young lady Charlie had failed to recognize had been located. The picture was gone. Someone had, obviously, taken it since he had been in the house yesterday afternoon.

*****

"You have any idea where these deposits came from?" Charlie asked. He was talking to the head teller, Bryan Westall, in Shannon's only bank. He had stopped by the bank just before lunch.

Bryan glanced through the record of deposits listed in Otto Hilty's bank book. He shook his head.

"Sorry, Charlie," he said. "There's really no way of telling where that money came from. There is no way to cross reference anything. You'd have to know …" A look settled over Bryan's face. He was quiet, but it looked like he was having a fight with himself, inside. One side finally won over the other, and he looked at Charlie with resolve.

"I'm not sure this has anything to do with what you're asking," he began, "but I just remembered something. I wait on Homer Schmidt when he comes into the bank, have for years, and …"

 He turned away to the shelf behind the teller window and began rummaging through a half dozen ledgers stacked there. When he found the record book he was looking for he leafed through the pages until he came to the one he wanted. He ran his index finger down the left side of the page and, when his finger stopped, he ran it horizontally across the page. Suddenly, he thrust the ledger through the teller window at Charlie.

"This is a record of Homer Schmidt's withdrawals for the past year," Bryan explained. "And this shows that Homer takes out the same amount, seventy dollars, around the ninth of every month."

Charlie just stared at the figures. He could not believe what he was seeing. And it wasn't just coincidence; couldn't be. For some reason, Homer was, in all probability, paying Otto Hilty seventy dollars a month, every month, like clockwork. What service could Otto possibly be rendering to Homer on a monthly basis that was worth seventy dollars?

Then he looked at it from the other direction: Charlie wondered what Otto knew about Homer Schmidt that allowed him to blackmail Homer. And he wondered if it was reason enough for Otto to be killed.

*****

Chapter Twenty

Homer Schmidt was a farmer on Shannon's west side. He owned a hundred and forty-five acres of farmland on Bixel Road that was tilled mostly with corn, soybeans, and wheat. He kept about thirty head of beef cattle and some hogs, for butchering.

He had lived in Shannon all his life, married a Shannon girl, Helen, and they had four kids. Homer's wife was a farm wife. She spent her days taking care of her family and their home. In spring and summer, she grew an enormous garden, as well as a dozen rows of sweet corn, and tended an orchard of fruit trees. The farm family lived on what they raised and grew. She canned the excess, or froze it, so they would have provision during the fall and winter.

The perfect winter's night, in Homer's estimation, was watching a John Wayne movie on television while munching on the popcorn and chocolate fudge with black walnuts Helen made in their big country kitchen. What made such nights extra special was savoring the homemade grape juice Helen had put up in the fall when the vines were laden with concord grapes. Life didn't get much better.

Shannon police were rarely seen in the countryside, so when Charlie Simmons called on Homer at his farm Monday just after mid-day Homer was more than a little curious.

"Afternoon, Homer," Charlie said.

Homer was sitting on the wooden slatted swing that hung from the ceiling of his wide front porch. He had just been thinking about heading out to the cattle barn when the policeman drove in his drive.

"Well, Charlie," Homer said. "You lost?" he joked.

Charlie managed a smile. An unspoken enmity existed between the townspeople and rural folk. Even though Charlie had been born on a farm and owned one, he had lived most of his life in Shannon. To the farmers he was one of *them*, a townie.

Charlie looked out on Homer's harvested fields, the stubble from the corn stocks providing a grim landscape. Smells from the livestock teased his nostrils; the sweetness of fermenting silage and aging cow manure competed for dominance. He heard an occasional 'clang' as a heavy metal lid dropped on one of the hog feeders. Raised squeals were a harbinger of a food fight between pigs.

"You hear about Otto Hilty being murdered at the livery barn in town Saturday night?" he asked Homer. Charlie thought he saw Homer start at mention of Otto.

Homer did not answer right away. Then, "I did." There was a pause. "You never know what will drive a person to do something rash, do you?" Homer hung his hands from the straps of his bib overalls by the thumbs.

"What's that mean, Homer? The killer was rash, or Otto?"

Homer kept his gaze level and replied, "I don't know anything about Otto being rash, but I'd say murderin' the SOB was a reckless thing to do."

Homer's slur of Otto prompted Charlie's next question. "Did you have a problem with Otto, Homer?"

Homer realized the mistake he had made calling the dead man an SOB. He slewed his eyes at Charlie. "Nope. No Sireee. I did not have a problem with Otto," he said.

"Where were you Saturday evenin', between eight o'clock and ten?"

Homer started at the question. "You ain't suspectin' me a killin' Otto?" he asked incredulously.

"Just answer the question, Homer," Charlie said.

"I was home, with Helen and the kids," he huffed.

Charlie nodded while he considered what Homer had said. He abruptly changed the subject. "You still a deacon at the Methodist church in town, Homer?"

"Have been for almost four years," Homer said proudly.

"The deacons oversee the money from the offering on Sundays, don't they?" Charlie pursued. He wasn't exactly sure where he was going with his questions. He was just following a hunch.

"What the hell's that supposed to mean, Simmons?" he asked. Charlie had hit a nerve.

"Just asking, Homer," he said. "Wasn't Otto a deacon in your church, too?"

Homer did not respond. Instead, he got up from the swing and headed out to the cattle barn. He was fuming. Charlie watched him as he walked away. He thought maybe his hunch had fleshed out a bit.

*****

Chapter Twenty-One

When Homer reached the safety of his cow barn and was out of Charlie Simmons' sight he swore angrily. "That damn Simmons!" he hissed. "And that damn Otto Hilty!"

Just over eighteen months ago Homer had taken ill with a nasty flu bug and had been laid up in bed for a whole week. He had missed going to church on the Sunday but was back the following week to take up his duty as deacon in charge of the Sunday collection plate.

Otto Hilty had filled in for Homer the Sunday he was out sick. Otto had counted and certified the amount of the collection, and seen it deposited in the bank first thing Monday morning. But he had not stopped there. He had noticed a sizable discrepancy between the previous Sunday's collection and the one he had just processed. This current Sunday had showed more than a ten per cent increase in giving over the last week. In fact, going back three months showed about the same amounts for each Sunday except the current one.

Otto wondered at the congregation's sudden burst of generosity. It was not a holiday Sunday, or a special mission's offering. As far as he could tell it was just a regular Sunday, so why the significant difference in the amount collected? It puzzled him all week long.

Homer was back the next Sunday and, as expected, took his place as deacon in charge of the offering. He counted and certified the amount. Still curious, Otto glanced at the figures

Homer wrote for the amount of the collection and was stunned! The amount was about ten per cent less than the previous Sunday when he, Otto, had processed the collection. It was in line with the previous three-month period Otto had checked. He thought he understood the discrepancy in the amounts of the various collections.

Several weeks passed, with Otto continuing to assist Homer and the other deacons with the weekly tithes and offerings. When the collection had been processed at the end of the fourth Sunday after Homer's recovery from the flu Otto made his move. He waited for the other deacons to leave the room where the collection was counted, closed the door, and confronted Homer.

"How long you been a deacon at this church, Homer?" he asked.

Homer's chest puffed with pride. "Just under four years," he said.

"You been stealing from the offering the whole time, or is this just recent?" Otto asked.

Homer gaped at him. It took him a moment to speak. "What the hell you talkin' about, Hilty?" he rasped. His face had turned purple with rage, but fear was also present.

Otto forced a slight smile. "I've been watching you since you came back from your bout with the flu. The Sunday you were out I was in charge of the offering, and it was a good bit more than the usual take. It puzzled me, Homer. It really did. 'How,' I wondered, 'could there be so much more in the plate on that particular day?' And then you came back, and the amount dropped. Significantly, I might add." He smirked.

"You got nuthin', Otto," Homer almost shouted.

Otto motioned for him to keep his voice down. They were, after all, still in church.

"Really?" Otto asked. "Is that how you want to play it? 'Cause I've been keeping a record of the amount you've certified for the past four Sundays, Homer. Your figures don't tally with what I counted for the same time frame." He paused. "You've been stealing from God, Homer."

Homer was furious. He was also terrified. If it came out that he had been stealing from the church … from God … he would be a ruined man. Helen would never forgive him. He would lose everything: his wife, kids, farm, and his freedom. His family would never recover from such shame.

Homer started to speak but his voice cracked and out came an unintelligible croak. He was trembling; sweat beads popped out on his forehead. He was afraid his bowels would void.

"Not denying it, eh?" Otto asked. He said it as a gibe. Homer wanted to clobber him, wipe that smug smirk off Otto's dorky face. He started to take a swing, but Otto artfully dodged the half-hearted attempt to hit him.

Homer suddenly collapsed into a nearby chair; he held his head in his heads, all the while moaning and mumbling to himself. "Jesus God, what have I done? What have I gotten myself into? I can't go to prison … can't go to the pen …" He was working himself into hysteria.

"Prison?" Otto quizzed. "That's not what I had in mind, Homer. Not at all," he said, shaking his head.

Homer stopped his blubbering and peered up at Otto. He cleared his throat. "What … what do you mean, Otto?" he asked.

Otto gave Homer an indulgent smile and patted him on the shoulder. "You going to prison would do neither of us any good, Homer," he said. "No … no good at all. We are going to be partners, Homer, you and me. I'll be the silent partner. The partner who doesn't do anything. The partner who gets, let's say, seventy dollars a month, regular as clockwork, for keeping his mouth shut. How's that sound, Homer?"

Homer did not have a choice. He merely nodded. He would have to steal a tad more each week to help pay off Otto. He had fallen into a moral abyss; he was more afraid of Otto than he was of God or the law.

But now, Otto was dead, and with his death Homer could taste the possibility of repentance and freedom. He vowed to begin paying back what he had stolen from the church. He would do it in the form of increasing his tithe. A smile lit his face for the first time in eighteen months. To be redeemed; restored. Ahh! The prospect of getting right with God flooded his body, causing him to weep. He thanked God for whoever had murdered Otto Hilty.

*****

114

Chapter Twenty-Two

Shannon was buzzing about the disappearance of Katie Mohler, and about the five hundred- dollar reward her husband was offering for help in finding her. Five hundred dollars was not to be sneezed at, and the town was energized to look for her.

Small groups of people formed, almost spontaneously, to go out and hunt for the missing farm wife. Search parties could be seen at all hours during daylight walking the Mohler farm and nearby woodlands. Neighboring farms were not exempt from being searched, so the Gratz brothers had their farms paced off by search parties, as well.

Allen County sheriffs, various local police, and even the volunteer fire department took a turn at searching for Katie. Packs of kids scoured the farm and its buildings, calling out in the excitement. The hunt had become a game to them; to the adults, it was a social event, and they all coveted the large reward.

At first, everyone assumed Katie, fifteen years younger than Hiram, had simply had her fill of the old cob and run off. No one would have blamed her for it. Hiram was known for his angry tirades and strident intolerances. Neither Katie nor the daughter or granddaughter were allowed to dress in slacks or wear their hair in one of the more stylish short cuts.

"None of my women be a dressin' like a man while they live under my roof!" he had been heard to roar.

He never gave them a moment's rest, either. They worked from sunup to sundown, seven days a week. When the chores in the house were caught up, he made them head to the fields to pick up rocks so the plow shares wouldn't get broken or made them weed the bean and corn rows by hand with a hoe.

"Idle hands are the devil's playthings," he would remind them as he drove them on to more physical labor.

Katie became gaunt and went about with a look in her eye that made some feel like she had her sights set in the next world. She was rarely seen off the farm, except when she came to Shannon to sell extra eggs to the town's bakery. People were alarmed by the physical changes in her appearance.

"That ole bastard will be the death of Katie," several of the woman in town had said amongst themselves. "And sooner, rather than later."

*****

116

Chapter Twenty-Three

Charlie stopped by the bank Monday afternoon and summoned Bryan Westall to the end of the counter.

"Bryan, I'd like to see the deposit records for the Methodist Church here in town," he said. There was no way to make the request sound casual. Bryan was instantly curious.

"What for?" he asked.

Charlie threw him a warning look. "Just get me the records, Bryan," he said.

Bryan went through his stack of ledgers again, pulling out one and consulting the page tabs that divided the large book. He turned to a page half-way through the book, checked to make sure he had the right church, and turned the book over to Charlie.

"The deposits for the last two years start here," he said, tapping the page near the top.

Charlie shook his head. "I need for you to go back further than that. At least two more years," he said.

Bryan just looked at Charlie for a moment, then he nodded and went into the vault. He came back about ten minutes later, carrying a dustier version of the ledger of the one they had already examined. He plopped the book on the counter, wiped his hands on his handkerchief, and began flipping the over-large pages, scanning the name posted at the top of the page as he did so. He finally found the entry he wanted, double-checked the information, and turned the ledger around for Charlie to examine.

Charlie nodded. "You got someplace I can sit down and look at this thing?"

Bryan led him to a small room used for interviews and job reviews and left Charlie to himself.

Charlie started at the first Monday-morning deposit made by the Methodist Church four years earlier and worked down the list. The amount of the weekly entries ranged from $984.23 to $1116.00, ebbing and flowing, but there were no large deviations. Until March 17, 1952. From this date forward the weekly deposits were approximately ten percent less than previous entries.

Charlie summoned Bryan. "Now I need to see the other book, Bryan. The one with the more recent deposits."

He picked up the trail of deposits from where he had left off in the older ledger. The amounts stayed within the same range as earlier, until April 26, 1954. The amount of the offering on that Sunday spiked up significantly, then the following week it was back in line with the previous totals.

Charlie sat back, perplexed. The numbers told a story; he just needed to figure out what that story was. He headed over to the Methodist Church.

"Miss Edna," he said, addressing the church's secretary.

"Charlie Simmons. I haven't seen you in church for a while," she scolded. "And not even a Sunday."

"No, Maam," he said. Miss Edna always made Charlie feel like the backslider he was. He had a theory that church growth had plateaued when Miss Edna became secretary. She just did not effuse Christ's love. "Miss Edna, I need to see the records you have of your Monday morning bank deposits going back four years.

Miss Edna's eyes grew wide with surprise, and then narrowed in suspicion. "And just why do you need to do that, Charlie Simmons?"

Charlie would not be bullied by Miss Edna today. "Official police business, Miss Edna," he said, and left it at that.

Miss Edna's multi-layered chin jiggled like a turkey's wattle and she flushed red with irritation. She huffed and wheezed a bit, then went to a metal file cabinet and thumbed through the file tabs in a drawer marked 'accounting'. She pulled out a file and started to hand it over to Charlie but stopped.

"Now see here, Charlie Simmons," she reprimanded. "This here file is private business. I don't wanna hear any gossip buzzing around Shannon about the file from her fat, piggy hand. "Loud and clear," he church business. D'you hear me?"

That really pissed Charlie off. He grabbed the file from her fat, piggy hand. "Loud and clear," he said.

*****

119

. I don't wanna hear any gossip buzzing around Shannon about

Chapter Twenty-Four

Back in his office with the door closed Charlie methodically studied the church file on the offerings. He focused on the same time frame he had followed in the bank ledger. The main thing he was interested in was the person who had been in charge of each Sunday's collection. The file confirmed his suspicions.

Homer Schmidt had told him he had been deacon at the church for almost four years, which was why Charlie was looking specifically at that time frame. Sure enough. The decline in the amount of the offering coincided with Homer's becoming in charge of the Sunday collection. It was his signature on the weekly take.

Charlie skimmed through the entries until he came to April 26, 1954. When he saw who certified the offering on that Sunday, he cracked a smile. Otto Hilty's neat, tight signature was on the form. Now he knew the story behind Otto's blackmailing of Homer Schmidt.

*****

He found Homer in the barn, finishing up afternoon chores.

"What'd you do with the money you embezzled from the Methodist Church, Homer?" Charlie decided on the direct approach in confronting Homer. It paid off.

Homer goggled at Charlie; his eyes were wide with terror. He had been caught completely off guard and his guilt was obvious. He broke out in a sweat, and had trouble catching his breath.

"How…?" His voice cracked; his bowels twinged, ominously. "How did you find out?" His voice had fallen to a whisper.

Charlie did not respond; he just stood, looking at Homer. Tears were coursing down the farmer's cheeks, and his body began to shake. He pressed two balled fists to his streaming eyes, but they could not plug the dam that had been waiting to break.

When Homer finished blubbering Charlie repeated his question. "Homer, where's the money you stole?"

Homer blew his nose on a big red hankie and dabbed at his eyes. When he was somewhat composed and sure his voice would be steady, he replied, "I bought a tractor."

Charlie said nothing, and Homer continued. "It was either that or quit farming. I babied my ole' Model A along's best I could, but it was used when I got it and there jist wasn't anything more could be done for it." There was a long silence. Homer looked pleadingly at Charlie. "What're ya gonna' to do, Charlie?"

Charlie thought long and hard.

"I'd like to say it's between you and the Good Lord, Homer," he said. "But it's not. You need to go talk to Pastor Hulhmann and tell him what you've done. All of it. Including the blackmail goin' to Otto."

Homer nodded. He feared this would ruin him and tar his family.

*****

Chapter Twenty-Five

Blanche Gruman sprawled on the park bench in front of the Presbyterian Church Tuesday enjoying the afternoon sun, her long, tanned legs stretched out on the sidewalk in front of the bench. She looked serene, with her face turned sunward, eyes protected by aviator sunglasses. Her blonde hair was almost white, bleached by the sun, and she wore it long and loose.

"Afternoon, Blanche," Charlie said as he made his way toward town hall.

Blanche turned her head to see who had spoken. "Well, hey, Charlie!" she replied. She quickly sat up, pulling her bare legs primly under the edge of the bench. It was a lady-like move; just what you would expect from Blanche. A broad smile, showing perfect pearl-white teeth lit up her face.

Blanche Gruman owned and operated a successful hair salon in town. For Shannon, it was an exclusive salon. Blanche was an excellent cutter and stylist, and her flamboyant but tasteful sense of style attracted the cream of Shannon's women to her salon, as well as some of the more prominent men. She had expanded her business over the course of a decade, hiring additional staff, but she was the queen bee, and closely guarded her select clientele.

Blanche had never married, though she had had a fairly constant parade of suitors. Rumor had it that when someone had once asked her why she had never married she had flippantly replied, "Why marry one man when I can make so many happy?" Whether or not this was true, it was generally agreed that Blanche had a less traditional approach to relationships with men than her female contemporaries, and it was speculated that many of her female devotees who religiously came to Blanche for hair treatment did so as a means of keeping an eye on her latest paramour, primarily to make sure it wasn't a wayfaring husband.

"You look mighty pleased with yourself," Charlie said. He stood in front of her, blocking the sun from her eyes. She removed her sunglasses, hooking one of the templates on the V-neck of a snug knit top that accented her generous curves.

"It's a great day to celebrate life," she told him, "and that's just what I'm doing." Clearly, she was enjoying herself.

Charlie changed the subject. "You hear about what happened to Otto Hilty the other night?"

His question soured Blanche's mood noticeably. Her voice took on a hard edge when she responded. "*That* SOB …" she began. "I don't truck with what happened to Otto," she said, "but I'll not shed any tears for him." She put her sunglasses on and stood, facing Charlie. "Like I said … it's a great day to celebrate." She walked off leaving Charlie standing, literally, with his mouth agape.

*****

Blanche Gruman had moved to Shannon with her mom and grandma when she was nineteen years old. They made quite a stir when they arrived in town. Blanche was quite the looker, and her mother, Greta, was an older, more mature version of Blanche. In other words, Greta was a sexy forty-year-old, single and on the prowl, as they say. Miss Lillian, the grandmother, was an elderly man-eater, now in retirement. People in Shannon called them The Three Gruman Women, and usually winked when they said it.

Greta and Blanche bought a beauty salon in Shannon and went into business as a mother/daughter partnership. The Shannon News decided to run an article about the town's most recent residents, especially since they had also opened a new local business, so the editor sent young Tom Heiks around to do an interview for the paper.

It was Tom's first interview, so he was understandably nervous, especially considering his subjects. He went to the little red house on Vance Street where the ladies lived, not knowing what to expect. He was shown into the cramped living room and offered iced lemonade and shortbread cookies. Looking around the small room, he thought it odd that there were no family pictures. Just a small, stuffed dog on the floor next to the couch where he sat that he swore had once been alive.

Miss Lillian monopolized the interview, for the most part. Her daughter and granddaughter could barely get a word in edgewise. The old matriarch was full of herself. She sat ensconced on a ghastly carved mahogany throne armchair whose seat was upholstered in a vivid rose color. The art nouveau piece had what looked like an enormous carved wooden butterfly with a human face at the top of its back, behind where Lillian's head rested. It was hideous, and fascinated Tom.

Miss Lillian pratted on about their previous life in a small town outside Dayton, mentioning several times over that she had lost her husband in the first war and how she "bless my bones, was forced to use the intelligence the good Lord gave me," to support her young daughter. She never said what form this support had actually taken, which he also found odd.

Conversation had tapered off and the silence became awkward. Thinking of her advanced age and her health, Tom suddenly asked, "Have you ever been bedridden, Ma'am?"

Miss Lillian's eyes lit up and she replied, "Good heavens, yes, young man! Hundreds of times, and twice in the hay mow!"

Blanche gasped in astonishment.

"Mother!" Greta scolded.

Poor Tom, red and flustered with embarrassment, mumbled a hurried thanks for the interview and scooted out the door. Greta followed on his heels, arriving at The Shannon News office minutes behind him, demanding to speak with the editor.

"Mother can be so ornery at times," she said, her voice low. "She says things sometimes for effect, to shock. Her flippant response to Tom's question about being bedridden must NOT be in your published article. I'm sure you understand." And here she made an outrageous attempt to bat her eyes at the elderly editor, an act that physically made him recoil.

"Ah, hem," he said, "not to worry Miss Gruman. I'll check Tom's article before it goes to print."

Miss Lillian's bedridden comment spread like wildfire throughout Shannon by the gossip matrix indigenous to small towns long before the censored interview appeared in the paper. It was a story that was repeated the length and breadth of the community to the delight of the tongue-wagging mavens, who branded The Three Gruman Women as loose women. Speculation rose anew about their background, reputation, and means of support.

Within six months of the infamous interview Greta had run off with a salesman whose territory included frequent stops in Shannon. It was the third time she had pulled that stunt, only this time she stayed gone. Miss Lillian died soon after, leaving Blanche to shoulder on alone.

She struggled to keep the salon running. The gossip mongers were unkind and boycotted her business. Desperate, Blanche decided to use those same busybodies to grow her clientele. She never dated anyone local, but always seemed to receive well-heeled visitors at her home on weekends before heading out of town. The rumor mill went into high gear, speculating about her beaus and conquests.

An air of mystique surrounded Blanche. Her sense of style, not small-town, set her apart from her contemporaries. She was like the front cover of Vogue wherever she went: perfect figure, perfect hair, and perfect manicure. Her aloofness to Shannon protected her from its mean jealousy and drew its nosey denizens to her salon like moths to a flame, hoping to catch just a snippet of gossip about the femme fatale to feed into the rumor mill.

*****

Chapter Twenty-Six

The phone was ringing in Charlie's office when he walked in after his conversation with Blanche Gruman. He caught it on the last ring.

"Charlie Simmons," he said.

"It's Doc Steiner, Charlie. You wanted me to give you a call after the coroner completed his autopsy on Otto Hilty."

Charlie waited for Doc to continue.

"The cause of death was, of course, the bail hook in the brain. There was no other sign of trauma or injury. Stomach contents indicate he had eaten approximately an hour before death, and the meal consisted of shredded chicken, pickles, potato salad, blueberry pie, and possibly iced tea. There was no drug or alcohol residue."

"Sounds like the menu at the Mennonite Church community supper," Charlie said.

"My thoughts exactly," Doc concurred.

"How many hundred people, do you think, went through that fellowship hall on Saturday night?" Charlie asked Doc. He heard a sigh on the other end of the phone line.

"More than I'd care to count," Doc replied, "but you got to start somewhere. Get a hold of Melvina Dillman. She's the one who's always in charge of their kitchen. Maybe she or one of her assistants remembers something. It's a long shot, but sometimes they pay off."

*****

"You have a good turnout for the community supper this year, Melvina?" Charlie asked. He had stopped by the church to see if the kitchen supervisor was in later that afternoon and found her sitting at the large stainless-steel work area in the church kitchen sipping a cup of coffee. Her audaciously dyed red hair supplanted what would have definitely been graying tresses. Melvina was, after all, almost sixty years old. Her over-made-up face stopped just short of being clownish, but she had a good heart.

"Yes, Charlie, we sure did!" she exclaimed. "And my feet are still recovering from it." Charlie involuntarily glanced down at her feet, which were shod in big fluffy slippers.

"It's the baked, shredded chicken that draws them in, that and your homemade pies," Charlie told her.

Melvina's eyes twinkled. She never tired of receiving compliments about her chicken. The recipe had been in her family for generations and she kept it a secret, which added even more mystique to the chicken.

"We only did the two flavors of pie this year, instead of the usual three," she told him. "Couldn't get enough blueberries, for some reason."

"You didn't have blueberry pie on the menu Saturday night?" he asked.

She shook her head. "Just apple and blackberry. One of the ladies baked a couple of chocolate cakes to fill in," she said. "Me, personally, I think folks prefer the pies."

*****

'Well, damn!' Charlie thought. 'Where did Otto get his blueberry pie?' The only possibility he could think of was The Pine restaurant. He walked down Main Street and when he came to the restaurant, he pressed his face against the full-front plate glass window, looking inside. He went in and walked back to where Rolland Simmons was scraping down the grill in preparation for the supper traffic.

"Hey, Rolland," he said.

Rolland stopped his scraping and looked over his shoulder. "Hi, Uncle Charlie," he replied. He turned back to cleaning the grill's surface.

"Were you workin' here on Saturday evenin', Rolland?" Charlie asked.

Rolland nodded his head. "I worked the five-to-eleven shift that night," he said over his shoulder. "Why?"

"You remember Otto Hilty coming in here for a piece of blueberry pie on Saturday?"

Rolland stopped what he was doing and walked over to where his uncle stood. He nodded. "I served Otto a slice of blueberry."

Charlie wanted to throttle his nephew. "And you didn't think it was important to mention that to me, Rolland?" he almost shouted.

Rolland flinched, like he was ducking a missile being thrown at him.

"You may be the last person to have seen Otto before he was murdered, and that seems to me to be something pretty important." He lowered his voice, cleared his throat. "What time was he in The Pine that night?"

Rolland thought long and hard, so much so that his face looked like it hurt. Suddenly, he smiled. "Just past eight thirty. I remember, 'cause Joe Birknauer was in here telling a lie about somethin' or other and he was eatin' blueberry pie and Otto said it looked good and he'd have a piece, too."

"How are you so sure about the time?"

Rolland grinned. "That's the lie Joe was telling, Charlie … about how it wasn't really eight thirty but twenty thirty. Somethin' about time being told on a twenty-four-hour system in England or France. One of them countries. He's such an awful liar."

*****

Chapter Twenty-Seven

"He was having a piece of blueberry pie at The Pine at eight thirty, Doc," Charlie explained.

He had gone to see Doc Steiner after his brief chat with Rolland.

"Does that make sense? He's having pie, probably talking to folks in the restaurant, like folks do, which means he wouldn't make it over to the livery barn until after nine o'clock. In fact, Rolland says Otto was in the restaurant just past eight thirty, which would put it even later. Your report states the time of death occurred as early as eight o'clock."

Doc Steiner listened to Charlie's concerns. This new piece of information threw his time of death estimate into doubt. Doc was only a small-town physician, but he was highly experienced in forensics, having acted as a medical examiner for years in the US Army. His conclusions were generally not called into question, but even he had qualms about this case.

"I see what you mean, Charlie," he said. "I don't have a ready answer." He paused to gather his thoughts. "I checked for early rigor in the barn as soon as I arrived, just after eleven o'clock. His one eyelid (he grimaced remembering the bail hook) was in a semi-advanced state of stiffening, which begins about two hours after death. His body temperature indicated the same, due to loss of core body heat. I don't know what to tell you."

Charlie was frustrated; he had hit a snag in his investigation.

"Unless …," Doc said, half to himself. "Had Otto been moved before I got there?" he asked.

Charlie thought a moment and nodded. "I pulled him out of the straw so's I could see who it was."

"What was his exact position, Charlie?" Doc asked.

"He was on his back, buried under the straw. Why?"

Doc slapped his left palm with his fist. "That would account for an earlier onset of rigor," he said, "as well as slowing the loss of body heat." He paused, reflecting. "Which means Otto would more than likely have been killed closer to, say, nine thirty or ten. The straw would have acted as an insulator, preserving his body heat, and speeding up the process of rigor mortis, especially if he was also laying on straw and not the cold barn floor. His eating the pie later at The Pine, after supper at the church, would also be the reason for the pie being less digested than the rest of the stomach contents."

"So, Otto could have easily had his final piece of blueberry pie and arrived at the barn in time to get murdered well after nine o'clock."

"Given this new information, I'd say so, yes," Doc agreed.

*****

Chapter Twenty-Eight

Charlie had a hunch about Blanche Gruman's perceived enmity toward the late Otto Hilty. Her almost vicious outburst about Otto's death made Charlie wonder what had transpired between the two residents of Shannon. He also wondered if Blanche would be celebrating that night, as well.

Just after dark that Tuesday night Charlie camped out in the side yard of the Catholic Church, next to Blanche's house on Spring Street. Tuesdays were always quiet days at St. Mary's, so Charlie was not worried about being seen by parishioners going home after choir practice or communion. He hid in the hedge running along her driveway that divided the church property from Blanche's.

It was a school night, which meant the streets of Shannon were quiet except for the occasional dog barking or car horn tooting. A door opened and closed on the other side of Spring Street, followed by the sound of a car's engine starting up. Charlie squinted at his watch dial: nine o'clock. Tom Hermann was returning for the remainder of his second shift at the Shannon Meters factory after stopping home for supper. The street grew quiet, again.

Charlie's ears pricked up. He heard a car approaching slowly from the direction of College Avenue. It was a powerful engine that ran smoothly and quietly. Just before it reached Blanche's driveway the driver doused the headlights, then turned into the drive. After a few moments someone got out of the car and walked to Blanche's side door, located under the car port. The person knocked, once, the porch light flicked on, then immediately off again. The door opened, framing Blanche in the light from the kitchen.

"Darling!" the man at the door said.

Blanche was seductively clothed in a sheer, black, flimsy lace baby-doll top with matching pantaloons. Her blonde tresses, tangled suggestively, shone in the light from within. She grabbed the man's hand and pulled him inside. Her visitor let out a low moan, pulling her into a tight embrace. They kissed feverishly. When they came up for breath, the man turned to close the door; Charlie's heart raced when he saw who her night caller was: one of the Shannon Meters owners, Travis Hunt.

*****

The Shannon Meters Corporation was a mainstay of Shannon's employers. Founded in the early 1900's before Charlie was born, the Shannon Meters factory had been an important part of Shannon's economic development, employing many women during and after both world wars. It was, in fact, the patriarch of factories in Shannon and its owners, the two Hunt brothers, were very wealthy, respected members of the community.

Both brothers had married college sweethearts and had kids who attended the local schools. They were the elites of the day. The families were deeply involved with the local Presbyterian Church, and the wives filled community positions like sitting on the school board or hospital auxiliary. There was never a capital improvement passed for Shannon or zoning issue decided without first consulting the Hunts. That is just how big a deal they were in Shannon.

And here was Travis Hunt, the younger brother, porking Blanche Gruman. It was a revelation that would have shocked and rocked the community. Madge Hunt, Travis' wife, was a strong-willed woman. She would have taken Travis to the cleaners in a divorce. Such a divorce settlement would jeopardize the fortunes of both Hunt brothers, not to mention the monetary repercussions that would filter down to the community as a whole. The economic trickle-down effect would be far-reaching, throwing a lot of people out of work and putting tremendous strain on local business.

Charlie had nothing concrete to go on, but he suspected Travis was another of Otto Hilty's blackmail victims. That would easily explain the hundred-dollar-a-month deposit into Otto's bank account, although that amount would be pocket change to a Hunt. Without anything substantial, Charlie would not dare to question Travis.

He headed back to his office, hoping the crisp night air would clear his thoughts. Maybe he had it backwards. Maybe it was Blanche who was being blackmailed. She could easily afford the fifty dollars that appeared regularly in Otto's account. 'But why blackmail Blanche for fifty if he could tap a Hunt for twice as much?' Charlie wondered. There was only one way to find out.

*****

Chapter Twenty-Nine

Charlie dropped by the 'Do n' Dye' on Cherry Street Wednesday morning on the off chance he could get a haircut from Blanche Gruman. He was in luck.

"Don't you normally go to JD's, Charlie?" she asked conversationally.

Charlie started to nod. "Hold your head still," Blanche scolded him. "JD's has got to be more fun than listening to a bunch of women carry on. Why're you really here? Your hair doesn't need a trim."

Charlie looked Blanche dead in the eye vis-à-vis the large mirror before him. She waited for his reply, her scissors poised near his left ear.

He got straight to the point of his visit. "Otto Hilty was blackmailing several people in town, Blanche," he said. The color draining from Blanche's gorgeous face and her near collapse told him what he needed to know. He continued, "I suspect you or someone close to you was one of Otto's victims, and I need for you to tell me what you know."

Blanche hung her head for a brief moment. When she looked up her face was devoid of all emotion except one: fear. She tried to speak, but her voice failed. A large tear threatened to spill over her right eye's lid, but she willed it to stop, hovering on the edge of what could easily become a spillway if Blanche let go.

She found her voice. "Not here," she managed. 'Meet me across the street, at the bench in front of the church." She gave his hair a final comb through, blew the cut hair off his neck, whisked the hair cutting cape away from the chair where he sat and prepared to close her station. Charlie paid for his trim and let himself out. He walked leisurely across the street to the park bench and took a seat.

Blanche joined him several minutes later. She pulled out a cigarette and Charlie lit it for her; her hands were shaking. She took a long, deep drag and exhaled, fishing a piece of tobacco off her tongue with her elegantly sculptured fingertips.

"So," she finally said, turning toward him as she stomped out her cigarette, "what do you want to know?"

"Was Otto Hilty blackmailing you?" Charlie asked.

"No. Next question."

"Was he blackmailing Travis Hunt? Charlie asked.

That was the million-dollar question, and it got twice the value from Blanche's response. The wind went out of her like she had been punched in the solar plexus. She almost doubled over but caught herself. When she finally managed to look Charlie in the face, he felt pity for her. She had the terrified look of a wild, delicate animal caught in a trap. The trap was her love for Travis Hunt.

"I'll take that as a yes," Charlie said. "Look, Blanche, I'm really sorry about all this. What you and Travis have is no business of mine and I want to keep it that way. But I've got a murder on my hands and I need to get to the bottom of it."

"Travis wouldn't … didn't … kill Otto," she said.

"I'd like to believe that, but I'll need to talk to Travis separately. What about you, Blanche? Where were you, the night Otto was killed? Not that I think you could have pegged him with a bail hook …"

She looked truly miserable, almost bedraggled. "Home. Alone. Like usual." It was the first time he had ever seen Blanche Gruman look vulnerable, and it saddened him. "What Travis and I have, Charlie," she began, "is something I never thought existed until I met Travis. I know the folks here in Shannon think I'm some kind of floozy, and yeah, I've walked to the beat of my own drum. Didn't get married right out of high school. Don't have three kids." She paused, reflecting. "That wasn't for me, Charlie, the picket fence thing. And I hate like hell that Travis is cheatin' on Madge, but we love each other and that's just the way the chips have fallen."

"Where's Otto come into all this?" Charlie asked.

Her shoulders slumped. "That little shit opened some of my letters I sent to Travis at work. He just had to know who Blanche-the-Maneater was sending perfumed letters to, so he took to steaming them open at his home. Can you believe it? A Federal employee, trusted with the sacred duty of not tampering with the public's mail?" She shook her head, dazed.

She had become child-like, fragile. Charlie found himself wanting to protect her and could understand why Travis would fall for a dame like Blanche. Beautiful, smart, sexy, delicate. Not at all like the hard-nosed, self-sufficient broad everyone assumed she was.

"When Otto figured out what was going on he moved in like a shark. He'd actually photographed some of my letters to Travis and laid them all out on Travis' desk in his office like some kind of trophies. Which I guess they were, since they enabled him to extract money from Travis for his silence. Travis said Otto gloated, threatening to take the letters to Madge. *That* couldn't happen … the fallout from Madge finding out would have caused a major problem for lots of innocent people. So, Travis paid … and paid … but he didn't kill Otto, Charlie."

Charlie had two out of three of Otto's blackmail victims; he wondered who the third could be.

*****

Chapter Thirty

Brrrrinnngg! Brrrrinnngg! Joe Birknauer came whizzing toward Sadie Snook and her daughter, Molly, where they stood, mouths agape, in front of Harry Shalley's five-and-dime store on Main Street first thing Wednesday morning. The bell on Joe's bike gave him an air of urgency as he sailed along.

"Peg Birknauer, ew doddamned big liar," Molly called out, "tell me a big lie!" Joe never understood why she called him Peg.

Frank and Sadie Snook lived on the edge of Shannon in a poor section of town. Frank worked on the local railroad section. Sadie was a bit soft-headed. The couple had two daughters, Molly and Betsy. Molly had the same mental capacity as her mom; Betsy, the younger daughter, was normal.

Joe, a grown man in his mid-thirties and the nephew of Fred Birknauer, was a compulsive liar. He was known around town for the pleasure he took deviling people and telling them lies. Sadie and Molly were often seen together walking around Shannon, and the pair was a favorite tease for Joe Birknauer.

"Sister Sadie, Sister Molly," he replied, "I can't do it today. John Garrand died this mornin' and I gotta go and send a telegram." He sped off on his bike, a man on a mission.

The custom of the day was to take flowers to the home of the deceased, and people at the Snook's economic level usually resorted to cutting their own flowers and taking the simple bouquet to pay their respects. The Snooks cut what few flowers they had, mostly zinnias and marigolds, and pilfered a few stems of dahlias from their neighbor.

Later that morning Sadie and Molly put on fresh aprons and, carrying their flowers tied with a red string, they set off for the Garrand house on Riley Street. They hammered on the front screen door. When John Garrand opened the door to them their mouths dropped open.

Both women gasped, wondering if the man standing before them was real. Molly reached out to touch the man's shirt sleeve and drew her hand back abruptly.

"Jedus Twiste!" Molly blurted. "Ain't ew dead? That doddamned liar Peg Birknauer!"

John Garrand's face split into a wide grin. He motioned to the flowers Molly clutched in her hand. "Peg told you I was dead?"

Sadie and Molly nodded in unison.

"Well, I'm not."

Molly looked at the flowers starting to wilt in her hand. A pout formed on her lower lip.

"You goin' to give me your flowers, or not?" Garrand asked.

"Jedus Twiste, no!" she said, pulling back. "Ew ain't dead!"

*****

Joe Birknauer had just leant his bike against the lamp post in front of Shalley's five-and-dime and was chuckling to himself at the trick he had pulled on Sadie and Molly.

"Joe Birknauer," someone called, and he looked up to see Charlie Simmons heading his way. He tried to wipe the smirk off his face.

"Mornin', Sir," Joe said respectfully. It did not do to piss off the police, he'd learned. Some of them did not have a sense of humor, and it was best not to take a chance trying to pull something over on a cop.

Charlie stopped next to Joe and his bike. "Were you in The Pine this past Saturday night, having some pie?"

'Heavens!' Joe thought. 'How could Charlie possibly know that? Was he being followed?' The thought unnerved him.

Joe flashed a big smile. "Yes, Officer, I was."

"What time was that, Joe?" he asked.

His face clouded. "Uh …," he began, "uh, I'm not sure, exactly," he replied.

"Think, Joe," Charlie urged him. "You was goin' on about some different way a tellin' time …," he said, trying to jog his memory.

"Oh, yeah, I was." His face lit up as he remembered. "But it was the God's truth, Charlie, what I was sayin' …"

"What time, Joe?" Charlie said, interrupting him.

"Uh, why, uh, it was … right about eight thirty. Yeah, eight thirty, 'cause I was saying it was really twenty thirty in Europe." He was relieved to have remembered. He turned serious. "I'm not in any trouble, am I, Charlie? I was just havin' a bit of fun with everybody and …"

"No, Joe. No trouble at all. In fact, you've been a big help." Charlie started to walk away but turned back. "You see anybody hanging out by the delivery barn later that night, by any chance?"

Joe shook his head. "I didn't go out that way, but Dirty Doc's the person you want to ask about that, Charlie," he said. "He's been workin' nights at the IGA as their night watchman, just down from the barn. Anybody saw anything it'd be Doc."

Charlie clapped Joe on the shoulder, thanked him, and left.

*****

Chapter Thirty-One

Dirty Doc had already come and gone again from his breakfast at The Pine, so Charlie had to call on him at his little travel trailer in the town dump on the south side of town. Charlie left the patrol car just inside the entrance to the dump and walked back to Doc's trailer. He didn't want to take a chance puncturing a tire on the trash strewn randomly in the drive.

"Doc, you home?" he called when he was about fifteen feet from the trailer. He waited and started to call again when the door slowly opened and a grizzled, dirty face looked at him from the doorway.

"Who's it?" Doc asked, squinting into the sun.

"It's me, Doc. Charlie Simmons. Can we talk?"

Doc passed from the trailer to outside the trailer in a slow, fluid movement that gave Charlie the feeling he was a specter of some sort. He stopped several feet from Charlie, dressed in his grimy blue jean attire, smelling like an over-ripe melon gone bad. His corn cob pipe was clamped between his teeth, unlit.

"Match?" Doc asked.

Charlie fished in his shirt pocket and extracted a book of matches, which he tossed to Doc. Doc very deliberately lit a match and applied it to his pipe, sucking hard on the stem. When it was going to his satisfaction, he held the matches out to Charlie with a nod.

"That's OK, Doc," Charlie said. "You can keep 'em."

Doc nodded his appreciation and waited.

Charlie moved a few feet to his left, trying to get upwind of Doc to escape his body odor. He wondered if there were legal grounds for forcing someone to wash.

"You been working for the IGA as their night watchman, Doc?"

Doc gave a nod, then sucked his pipe.

"Were you working there this past Saturday night when Otto Hilty was killed?"

Doc nodded again.

"Did you see anybody that night, Doc, around the livery barn or behind any of the houses off the alley? Say between nine and ten thirty?"

Doc pulled the pipe stem from his mouth and looked down in the bowl to see if it was still going. He gripped the mouth of the stem in his teeth and sucked 'til his cheeks collapsed. When it was smoking the way he liked it he gave Charlie his attention.

"I did see someone leave the barn but don't know when. Don't wear a watch."

"Did you see who it was, Doc?" Charlie held his breath.

Doc shook his head. "Don't see distances," he said. "Need glasses. But he was a big feller. With a limp."

*****

Chapter Thirty-Two

The search for Katie Mohler had turned up no leads and no Katie. Hiram had upped the reward amount to a thousand dollars, which sent search parties out with renewed determination to find her. A thousand dollars was a princely sum of money.

Hiram's second farm, a smaller homestead just north of Shannon, had been included in the efforts and was also being scoured for any sign of the missing wife. Still, nothing. It was like she had just vanished into thin air. The deepening mystery sent more tongues wagging.

A small percentage of Shannon's residents suspected Hiram of doing her in, but most of the locals thought Katie had finally had her fill of her belligerent husband and his Tartar ways and run off with the Fuller Brush salesman that passed through town from time to time. More telling was that these same locals could not blame her for leaving and sympathized with her. But they also felt pity for old Hiram, who seemed inconsolable.

Just like after the Gratz brothers' barns burned, the town of Shannon settled back into its small town rhythms and routines, but the large cash reward offered was too big to forget and everyone seemed able to include a new search for Katie as part of their daily regimen.

*****

Charlie made an appointment to see Travis Hunt at the Shannon Meters plant in the middle of the morning on Thursday. He tried to make it sound like it was not police business to Travis' secretary, but she didn't buy it. When he showed up at the appointed time the secretary acted like she was in on some kind of conspiracy.

"I just need to talk to Travis about the traffic situation at the end of second shift," he told her. Her look said 'Sure,' but she did not believe that was the real reason for his visit.

Travis was seated at his desk, which was strewn with orders for the industrial parts the company manufactured. He looked up from his work as Charlie entered. He gave a terse smile.

'Blanche must a told him I'm on to Otto's blackmail,' he thought.

Travis stood and shook Charlie's hand, and gestured to a padded captain's chair in front of his desk. "Have a seat, Charlie." His tone was civil, but tense.

"I appreciate you taking the time to see me, Travis," he began. He changed tack. "Look, there's no point beatin' about the bush since I'm sure Blanche Gruman has told you why I'm here."

Travis' face grew pinched at mention of his paramour. He said nothing and waited for Charlie to continue.

"I'm not here to cause you any trouble, Travis," he said. "I'd like to promise you that no one need hear of the relationship between you and Blanche, and I'll do everything in my power to keep that quiet, but look here, Travis, I've got a murder I need to solve and you and Blanche are persons of interest in my inquiry."

Travis leaned forward in his chair; his face had become an angry mottled red. "Now YOU look here, Charlie Simmons," he spat. "You know who *I* am in town. I can have that tin badge yanked off your chest," he snapped his fingers, "like that. Don't you come in here throwing accusations around. No, Sir! Don't you dare!"

Charlie was unflappable. "Travis, Blanche has told me about Otto and the blackmailing. And she's told me about the two of you. Like I said, I don't want to cause you problems; I just want to get to the truth and find out who murdered Otto."

Travis realized his bluff had failed, and his head dropped to his chest. He was still for several seconds, then his head started to slowly wag back and forth.

Charlie spoke softly. "You were paying Otto a hundred dollars a month, weren't you, Travis?"

Travis nodded.

"You've been doling out blackmail money to him since 1953?"

Travis looked up in surprise, his mouth dropped open. "How did you …?" he began.

Charlie waved him to silence. "I found Otto's bank book and checked with the bank for his deposit records." Travis let out a strangled cry. "Don't worry, Travis," he assured him. "I haven't divulged the names of the people Otto was extorting, nor do I intend to." He paused, but he had to ask the next question.

"Travis, where were you this past Saturday night between nine and ten thirty?"

For a moment, defiance flashed over Travis' handsome face, but the passing look was replaced by resignation. "At home," he whispered. "I was home with Madge and the kids."

Charlie let himself out of Travis' office. His secretary, with a flustered look on her face, busily sorted through a stack of papers she had dropped on the floor.

'No doubt listening at her bosses' door,' he thought, and hoped to hell it was soundproofed.

*****

Chapter Thirty-Three

Charlie still had another blackmail victim to find. He had pretty much ruled out Homer Schmidt and Travis Hunt as Otto's killer, and needed to find victim number three. He called on Doc Steiner in the hopes that their joint thinking might come up with a piece of information, no matter how small, that would steer him in the right direction with the investigation.

He found Doc in his office on Kibler Street. The physician had just returned from making a house call on one of his expectant mothers and he was restocking his doctor's satchel.

"People never cease to amaze me, Charlie," Doc said. "Tom and Rachel Winkler are expecting their first child any day now." He shook his head, then continued. "I remember they'd been married almost a month and Tom stopped me on the street one day, just full of himself. "Doc," he says, "we'll be calling on you one of these days. My wife and me, we done somethin' last night."" He paused. "How could that be, Charlie?" he asked. "Almost a month had gone by since they were married, and they just figured out what it was all about. Is that even possible?"

"Tom and Rachel are good people," Charlie said.

"None better," Doc hastened. "Fine people, but heavens!" he said. "Tom was brought up strict by his mama; I guess Rachel had to finally teach him the moves." He chuckled.

Charlie got around to his reason for stopping by. "I'm stumped, Doc," he said. "I discovered Otto was blackmailin' several people in town. I found out who two of his victims were, and I've talked to them, but I don't think they had anything to do with Otto's murder. According to Otto's bank book, he had three people he was squeezing money out of. I've found two but have no idea who the third person is. Whoever he is, he's been paying Otto fifty-five dollars a month since 1952. That adds up to a heck of a lot of money, Doc."

Doc had grown quiet and still listening to Charlie. "It's me, Charlie," he said, at last.

Charlie thought he had misunderstood. "What did ya say, Doc?"

"Me." Doc said, again. "I'm the third blackmail victim Otto was fleecing."

Charlie couldn't help it; his jaw dropped. "Doc," was all he said.

Doc's shoulders sagged; his arms hung loosely by his side, his head slumped on his chest, then he looked up at Charlie.

"It happened when Otto's mama was sick and dying," he explained. "My God, she was in such pain! The cancer was eating her alive and she was out of her mind in agony." He grimaced at the memory. "She begged me to help her die, Charlie. Day after day, pleading, suffering so. There was no hope, at all, of her living. It was just a matter of days, and the pain medicine wasn't alleviating her torment. She said no one would ever know … that it would be a mercy in God's eyes to help her to die. So, I did."

"Did what, Doc?"

"I helped the poor woman to her eternal rest, Charlie. That's what I did."

"How? And what does that have to do with Otto blackmailing you?"

"I left an extra ampule of morphine on her bed stand one day. She just went to sleep and never woke up. Her son, Otto, saw the extra empty ampule and he knew I'd done it. He threatened to report me, but blackmailed me, instead."

"Good God, Doc," Charlie said. "He used his mother's death as a means of extorting money from you?" Charlie shook his head, "You live around people all their lives and still have no idea who they really are."

After he'd said it he wondered if he meant Otto Hilty or Doc Steiner. He had worked with Doc for years, and never would have guessed he had anything to hide or that he had fallen prey to blackmail. As for giving Mrs. Hilty extra morphine so she could escape the agony of her death, it was understandable. Charlie could not imagine tending terminally ill patients and the toll it would take on a person. Understandable, but that did not mean it was the right thing to do. Still, he would not be Doc's judge.

"It's time for me to retire, Charlie," Doc was saying. "I violated my Hippocratic oath." He suddenly looked old and haggard.

"Why, Doc, you can't retire. Who's going to be this town's doc if you quit?" He still recalled how Doc Steiner had done the first appendectomy in town and what a big deal it had been, to cut a man open and then sew him back up. And Doc had taken out Charlie's tonsils when he was twelve. He remembered sitting on the kitchen table at home, holding the drip pan under his chin while Doc cut them out.

Doc didn't respond.

"Doc?" Charlie waited for Doc to look up. "I have to ask you this: where were you on Saturday night between nine and ten thirty?"

Doc thought a moment. "Up to the hospital," he answered. "Stella Lehman was just giving birth to a baby girl. I left her bedside when I got your call about Otto."

Charlie nodded. He had his three out of three, but none of them seemed candidates for Otto's murder.

*****

Chapter Thirty-Four

"You find the key to Otto Hilty's safe deposit box, Charlie?"

Charlie had stopped in the bank just after noon to cash a check when the head teller, Bryan Westhall, approached him.

Charlie's face showed surprise. "Why, no, Bryan," he replied. "Otto had a safe deposit box here in the bank?"

Bryan nodded. "He opened one about four years ago," Bryan told him. "He should have a key for it at his house somewhere," he added.

Charlie nodded his thanks and decided to pay a visit to Otto Hilty's house again.

*****

The key was taped inside the backing of the picture of Otto's parents sitting on Otto's desk. On a small ring with a tag attached to the key was written the number 322. Charlie pocketed the key and set out for the bank.

Bryan Westhall had Charlie sign the safety deposit ledger and escorted Charlie into the bank's vault.

"Box number 322," Charlie said, holding the key he had found at Otto's place.

Bryan produced the bank's master key and, inserting the two keys in the locks on box number 322, unlocked the safe deposit box. He lingered while Charlie pulled the box from its slot.

"You got a place where I can look through this thing?" Charlie asked, holding the box.

 Bryan nodded. "Right this way, Charlie," he said, leading him to a small cubicle with a door. Bryan opened the door for Charlie and stood aside as Charlie entered the private space. Charlie set the box down, turned, and closed the door. Bryan sighed. This was the most excitement he'd had in years.

*****

To say the contents of Otto Hilty's safe deposit box caught Charlie by surprise is a mastery of understatement. There were some odd bits of dated jewelry, obviously from his mother, along with a life insurance policy with a death benefit in the amount of ten thousand dollars. Given that Otto had no relatives that Charlie knew of, he wondered who the beneficiary was. Glancing through the document he found that, in the event of Otto's demise, the money would go to the nursing home in the community. A worthy cause, Charlie thought.

The most notable documents in the box were a small stack of brand spanking new bearer bonds that totaled a hundred thousand dollars. The amount took Charlie's breath away! "Where, in the name of Glory, did Otto Hilty get the dough for these bearer bonds?" he asked aloud. He sat back, trying to process this latest discovery and what meaning it could have regarding Otto's murder.

160

Charlie was not slow; he was methodical. He sat up and slapped his thigh. There was a fourth blackmail victim somewhere out there, he concluded, and he had no idea who it could be, but he sure as heck would try his darndest to find out who else Otto had been threatening with exposure.

The one remaining item in the safety deposit box was an unsealed enveloped containing a half dozen pictures, hastily taken and out of focus, of some old bottles. Charlie glanced quickly through several of the photos without thinking and stuffed them back in the envelope. He left the contents of the safe deposit box exactly as he had found them, opened the door to the waiting Bryan, and the two men locked the box back in its secure vault.

"You keep a record of everybody who accesses these safe deposit boxes?" Charlie asked.

Bryan nodded. "Every time someone wants in their safe deposit box they have to sign in on a sheet, which I or one of the other tellers then dates and signs."

"And it takes the two keys to get in the locked box?" Charlie asked.

Bryan nodded.

"When was the last time Otto looked in his box?" Charlie wanted to know.

Bryan scanned through several pages in the sign-in ledger. "According to this," he said, pointing, "he signed in seven months ago."

"You mean he hasn't been in his strong box for seven months?"

"Looks like it," Bryan said.

"Hmmm," was all Charlie had to say to that.

*****

Chapter Thirty-Five

The loafers in JD's barber shop Thursday afternoon were listening to Turley Rupright tell a story about Sankie Fenton when his voice was changing years earlier.

"Sankie stood at the counter in my grocery store and says, "I want a loaf of bread **and a pound of butter**."" The first half of the sentence Turley had done in falsetto, the second half, in bass. "And I said, "Give me a minute and I'll be up to wait on both of you.""

Turley had told the tale dozens of times over the years sitting in JD's, but no one ever complained. They all sniggered politely and smiled. Turley turned his attention to Charlie.

"Any news on the whereabouts of Katie Mohler, Charlie?" he asked.

Charlie shook his head. He was frustrated that no progress had been made in locating the missing wife of Hiram Mohler. "No, Turley," he replied.

"It's a darn shame," Turley said. "She always seemed all alone in the world. No relatives or nuthin' …"

"That's not exactly correct," Lazarus Bassinger interrupted. "Katie's aunt and uncle raised her here in Shannon after her folks died from influenza."

Charlie's ears pricked up. "Who were her people, Lottsie?"

"Why, Broman and Janie Rose Hilty," he said.

"Otto's parents?" Turley asked.

Lottsie nodded.

"Then Otto was Katie's cousin?" Turley asked.

Lottsie nodded, again.

"Was she, by God!" Charlie exclaimed. This piece of information was significant, he knew, but did not know where to piece it in. He struggled, trying to remember.

"Broman never came home from the war, poor soul," Lazarus said. "I heard he got a direct hit from one of Hitler's shells. Wasn't even nuthin' to send back in a box. It was real hard on Janie Rose."

"We shot a volley over the Hilty house on Armistice Day in 1945," Turley recalled. He shook his head as the memory flooded his thoughts. "What a day that was! Factory whistles blew, church bells rang, and people in town formed a parade that marched up and down every street in town carrying the Stars and Stripes. When they came to a house that had a white flag with a blue star in the window or a white flag with a gold star, they fired a volley over the roof. A blue star meant there was a boy in service; a gold star meant 'killed in action'. We shot five volleys over Bertha Stalling's house … she sent five boys off to that damn war. I remember the picture the Shannon News ran of her five grown sons standing 'round her when they came back home."

*****

Chapter Thirty-Six

The next couple of days in Shannon were, mercifully, uneventful. The last of the crops in the surrounding farms had been harvested and stored, and the first barn raising to replace Clyde Gratz' barn had taken place, with another barn raising scheduled for his brother, Tom. Life had pretty much returned to the normal ebb and flow of a small town.

Dirty Doc was sporting a new set of blue jean clothes, which perked everybody up who crossed paths with him. The old set, grimy and stiff with dirt and rancid perspiration, had ended up in the dump.

There was a minor incident on Friday afternoon when Charlie Sweet tried to knife Richard Clay, but Rolland Simmons warned Richard off, averting a catastrophe.

Charlie Sweet lived in the town's 'bachelor house', a house just behind the Presbyterian parsonage that had been divided up into rooms and let out to unmarried men. Charlie went about scowling all the time, never smiled. He was meaner than a bear with a sore ear, and Richard Clay, a lad of fourteen, teased him relentlessly.

On this particular Friday Charlie Sweet figured he'd had enough of Richard. He saw the young man walking up Cherry Street, toward Main, and hid in the hedge of the Presbyterian Church that ran along the sidewalk. Richard would pass by where Charlie hid, and Charlie had a burning anger and a sharp knife waiting for him.

Rolland Simmons saw old man Sweet crouched down in the bushes, brandishing a knife, and he also saw Richard Clay heading his way, like a lamb to the slaughter.

"For Christ's sake, Richard, run!" Rolland yelled. "Charlie Sweet's hidin' in the bushes along the sidewalk and he's got a knife, ready to stab ya!"

Richard scrambled across Cherry Street at Rolland's warning. Charlie Sweet stood up, knife in hand, gnashing his teeth at Richard. Then he turned to glare at Rolland.

"That'll be all, Charlie Sweet," Charlie Simmons told him, from behind. He had seen Sweet acting suspiciously and, at Rolland's warning, moved in to stop Sweet from trying to kill Richard Clay.

"And you, Richard Clay, you quit a teasin' this old man or one of these days he just might slit your young throat."

Richard blanched at the thought and ran off.

Rolland was heading back to The Pine to work his grill shift for the evening meal. Charlie walked with him, enjoying the quiet of a Shannon fall afternoon when the light was just starting to turn everything to a mellow gold. They came upon a dark green Chrysler New York Deluxe car parked in front of Bott's hardware store. The chrome highlights were polished to a sheen that almost made your eyes water in the sunlight. The two men stopped to admire the car. It had an Indiana license plate.

"Geez, Charlie," Rolland gushed. "Have you ever seen such a beaut of a car?" His eyes lovingly wandered over every inch of the grand touring car.

His admiration was cut short by a snarling, growling bulldog chained to the thick, velvet pull rope that ran along the back of the front seat. The back windows were open on both sides of the car. The dog's chain ran freely along the rope so he had full use of the back seat and could thrust his massive head out the window. Rolland jumped back when the dog menaced him.

"Dang! I didn't see him in there. Scared me," Rolland said. The dog, sensing Rolland's discomfort, barked sharply, snapping his powerful jaws. The animal carried on for several minutes, getting bolder and more vicious by the minute. The chain grated against the side of the door as he lunged to get at Rolland, who had backed up, scared by the animal's savagery.

"That is one mean dog!" Rolland said, backing up still further.

Charlie had been silent the whole time, watching the dog's malice escalate. Suddenly, Charlie charged the car, roaring at the dog through the open window. The dog let out a yelp of terror, scuttling to the far side of the car, where he cowered in fear at the human who had called his bluff.

Charlie walked off, grinning. Rolland stood, amazed. His Uncle Charlie was something else.

✳✳✳✳✳

Chapter Thirty-Seven

October 2, 1943 had been a day of traumatic change for the town of Shannon. In a close-knit community where everybody knows everybody and many people are related to each other, the deaths of four young men from four prominent Shannon families in one fell swoop is a staggering blow to a small, rural village. Even though the incident had taken place years earlier, the painful memory of the loss still lingered.

Wade Amstutz, Corey Diller, Arthur Roney, and Seth Weaver had graduated from Shannon High School the previous spring and all had taken jobs in the nearby city of Findlay. Wade had been captain of the high school football team and lettered in three sports. Corey had been a regular in the high school's drama productions. Arthur was the only son of Stillman Roney, Shannon's bank president, and had decided to work a year before enrolling in university. Seth had also played sports, was senior class president, and had been escort to Shannon's homecoming queen his senior year.

On their way home from work that Friday evening of October 2nd Arthur had been driving the new Packard Cavalier Touring Sedan his father had bought him as a graduation present. It was the only one like it in Shannon, with its signature chrome side spear trim, white wall tires he kept immaculate, and Carolina Cream paint job. The car was gorgeous, and Arthur drove her like a racehorse.

It was a big football game night in Shannon, as the yet-undefeated home team faced its primary rival and historical nemesis. The young men were excited about the game and had been celebrating with open bottles in the car as they headed home. The Packard was a heavy car, but it was no match for the Lake Erie and Western locomotive that tore into it at Hewell's Corner where the railroad crossed Old Highway 25 north of town.

The four young Shannonites were killed, instantly. After a brutal impact, the iron behemoth pushed the car along the tracks for a mile until it came to a complete stop, with the car wedged part-way under the engine. The point where it came to rest was another rail crossing, Gratz' Crossing. The Packard was no longer a chariot; more a rag doll with flat tires, crushed in roof, and frame bent nearly in two.

Otto Hilty happened on the scene where the train had finally stopped. He was on his way back to Shannon after a trip to a nearby town where he'd been to purchase a new camera. He was dumbstruck at the carnage before him, and quickly exited his car to see if he could be of any assistance. What he saw truly sickened him.

The car he recognized right away, so he assumed the driver was young Roney, though the figure at the wheel was mangled and damaged beyond recognition. The front seat passenger had been Wade Amstutz. Otto knew this by Wade's decapitated head resting precariously on the dashboard. The rear seat passengers were mutilated and in pieces. Blood was everywhere.

Otto tried to open the driver's door, but it was jammed. He peered in the side window and saw several open bottles of booze, now empty, on the front seat and floor. He hesitated, then went back to his car and fetched his new camera, loaded with film and ready to go. His conscience pricked him for all of five seconds at what he was about to do, then he went ahead and did it anyway. He could not help the car's occupants, and this was an opportunity he did not want to let go by.

He snapped a couple of pictures of the car from the outside, then focused on some shots of the car's grisly interior. He cut his picture taking short when the train's engineer blasted him with a pull from the engine's whistle and shook his fist at him from the engine's door. It would not do to get caught at what he had just done, so he hopped in his car, turned around in the road, and sped off.

*****

The decimated Packard was put on a flatbed, transported home to Shannon, and left in the parking lot behind the Ford garage on Cherry Street. The morbidly curious in Shannon, and there were plenty of them, would stop by to gape at the bloodstained, flattened car. Their gruesome inquisitiveness would be rewarded by glimpsing an odd, solitary torn shoe lying on the floor of the rear seat, or the shattered windshield where Wade Amstutz's head had cracked it before he was decapitated.

It was a somber testimony to the fleetingness of life, and in some esoteric way the car helped the citizens of Shannon come to terms with the horrific death of four of their finest young

171

men. It became a makeshift memorial to the town and helped the community to grieve.

*****

Chapter Thirty-Eight

Friday afternoon Charlie went to the bank with Otto's deposit box key to have another look in the box. He duly signed the ledger and Bryan West brought the bank key and the two men used their keys to free the box from its pigeonhole in the vast bank of boxes.

As before, Charlie took the box to the little cubicle and closed the door. He opened the box and stared. He double-checked the box's number, 322, and looked in the strong box, again. The bearer bonds were gone! All one hundred thousand dollars' worth of them.

He opened the door to the cubicle. Bryan was standing, waiting to put the box back in the vault, but one look at Charlie's face told him something was very wrong.

"Who's been in this safety deposit box since I was here yesterday?" Charlie demanded. His gruff, powerful voice alarmed Bryan.

"Why, no one," Bryan said. "They couldn't, not without the key …."

"Well, by God, someone's been in this box," Charlie said, his voice rising. "And they stole something from it."

Charlie stormed over to where the sign-in ledger was kept and thumbed through it. No one had been in the vault to look at any of the safety deposit boxes since yesterday's visit to the bank.

"Who's in charge of this ledger?" he demanded of Bryan.

"Well, well, I-I-I am," he stammered. His face was red with embarrassment, his eyes wide with fear. He had never seen Charlie worked up like this, and it was frightening to behold.

Charlie's eyes narrowed. "The other day, Bryan, you told me it took the two keys to open Otto's box: the one I took from his desk, and the one you have." Bryan nodded his head, agreeing. "Bryan, does anyone else have a duplicate of the key I have?"

Bryan shook his head. "No. Oh, no Sir!" he said. "No one could have that key. Only the person who rented the box. Only one key was given out, on account of only Mr. Hilty rented the box. Just for himself. He never signed anyone else on to his safe deposit box account." He continued shaking his head.

"You said only one key was given out, Bryan. Was there a second key available that stayed in the bank?"

Bryan was struck dumb. Slowly, he nodded his head.

"And where would that key have been kept?" Charlie wanted to know.

"Well, in the locked bottom drawer of this desk," he answered.

"And who has the key to that desk drawer?" Charlie persisted.

Bryan's face colored. "Why, everyone who works in the bank, I guess."

This was a new and delicate wrinkle to the case, and Charlie needed time to think. He went back in the cubicle and gathered

the remaining items in Otto's box to take with him. He turned
back to Bryan.

"Uh, Mr. Simmons," Bryan said, "Sir, you can't just take Mr.
Hilty's things out of the bank."

Charlie turned and studied the determined look on Bryan's
face. "You're right, Bryan," he said. "Let's do this. You write
me a receipt for these items and date it, and I'll sign for it. That
way, you'll have a record that I've taken them, OK?"

Bryan thought a moment. "I maybe should ask Mr. Roney if
that's OK," he said.

"No, Bryan," Charlie responded. "I want this to stay between
the two of us, understand? I don't want you to mention what
has happened to a soul. I mean that. I'll hand write an
explanation exonerating you of any blame, just in case
something happens, but it won't. Trust me."

Bryan was not comfortable with Charlie's suggestion, but
Charlie was the law, and he realized that he had no other
choice.

*****

Charlie carried the contents of Otto's safe deposit box back to
his office in a bank bag Bryan had provided. He locked his
door and spread the few things out on his desk. Some old
jewelry and some pictures of old bottles. What a haul.

He pawed through the trinkets absent-mindedly, then shuffled
through the pictures. Old bottles. Why would anyone take a
picture of an old whisky bottle? He looked closer at the

photos, and suddenly realized what he was looking at. It was a picture taken of the inside of a car with an empty bottle lying on the front seat and a hand next to it in an unnatural position. Part of a man's leg was also visible. It was difficult to make out because the picture had been taken through the car's window and a reflection from the glass made it confusing. He flipped to the next picture, which showed much the same thing, only this time there was a leg on the other side of the seat where the bottle lay, and what looked like a pool of blood.

"What the hell is this?" he said to himself.

The next to the last picture was the one that explained the whole thing. It was a picture of a cream-colored Packard Cavalier Touring Sedan, partially crushed under the front of a locomotive.

*****

Chapter Thirty-Nine

Charlie sat across the desk from Stillman Roney, Shannon's bank president, in Stillman's office. The photographs Charlie had taken from Otto Hilty's safe deposit box were spread out on the top of Stillman's desk.

"It was you, wasn't it, Stillman, who broke into Otto Hilty's safe deposit box and removed the bearer bonds?"

Stillman was standing with his back to Charlie, gazing out the window of his office that looked onto Church Street. He said nothing for several moments. Charlie wondered if Stillman had heard him. He finally turned away from the window and sank into his leather desk chair, swiveling toward Charlie. He stared at Charlie, not seeing him.

Charlie spoke again, this time more gently. "Stillman, did you know there was alcohol involved in your son's death?"

Stillman bowed his head, his shoulders slumped. "Yes," he said in a voice not much louder than a whisper. He was a defeated man. "Yes," he said, louder. He looked Charlie square in the face. "I knew."

Charlie was silent, thinking about what it meant. "Did Stoney know?" he asked, referring to the previous police chief who had been in office when the tragic accident occurred.

"Yes, he knew," Stillman said. "He stopped by right after it happened and told me he'd found open bottles of booze in Arthur's car and how did I want to handle it." He paused. "I told him …" His voice broke. "I told him I'd appreciate it if Arthur's name wasn't tarnished by the fact that he'd been driving under the influence of alcohol and responsible for the deaths of the three other young men in the car."

Stillman had been kneading his hands together feverishly and, when he realized what he was doing he stopped, placing his hands on the desktop. They looked like fish out of water, so Stillman tried holding them in his lap, but they would not be still.

"So, Stoney falsified his police report?" Charlie asked. This was probably a contributing reason to Stoney's tenure as police chief being cut short. His early death had been brought on by a heart attack.

Stillman nodded. "Yes," he said.

There was a lull in the conversation, and then Charlie popped the big question. "Did you murder Otto Hilty because he was blackmailing you?"

The question took Stillman by complete surprise. "Lord, no!" he blurted. "You seriously don't think I had anything to do with what happened to Otto!" The very idea left the bank president aghast. "Otto wasn't blackmailing me any longer," he added. "Our agreement was a one-time payoff. A hundred thousand in bearer bonds. That was our arrangement, and Otto stuck to it. He never came back to me for more money."

"And the lawsuit against the railroad? It was based on a lie, Stillman. That's insurance fraud."

Stillman sat with his head hanging. He was at a loss for words.

"Did Stoney know you intended to sue the railroad over the accident?" Charlie asked.

The man sitting in the president's chair shook his head. "I decided to do it after Stoney passed on," he said. "I was angry and wanted somebody to pay for what happened to my boy, even if it was his fault."

"Did you keep the money from the settlement?"

Stillman was almost offended by the question, but backed off, shaking his head. "I took out the hundred grand for Otto and gave the rest to several AA chapters around here. I didn't want or need the money; I just wanted justice," he answered.

Charlie was conflicted. He believed that Stillman had not been involved with Otto's murder, but there was still the matter of defrauding the railroad company's insurer. He had known Stillman Roney for three decades, two of which Stillman had served as president of Shannon's only bank. He was a good and decent man, albeit a bit snooty, but he had served the community well and was highly thought of. He could not see what good it would do to arrest him at this late date, ruin his reputation, and deprive the community of his steady leadership. It just did not seem a proper way to repay a man who had given so much to Shannon.

Charlie stood to leave. "Between you and me, Stillman, put that hundred thousand in bearer bonds to good use somewhere it'll do a lot of good."

*****

179

Chapter Forty

Later that afternoon Charlie made yet another trip to Otto Hilty's snug little cottage on Jackson Street. Something Blanche said had been niggling at him, and with the discovery of the photographs in Otto's safe deposit box the niggling had turned into a definite question mark.

He let himself in and headed to the kitchen. A door from a small alcove just off this area was what he was looking for. When he opened the door the cool, musty air from the basement assailed his nostrils. Charlie flipped on the light switch on the wall just inside the stairwell and clambered down the steep, wooden steps.

He glanced around the room at the bottom of the stairs: water heater, furnace, wash machine, indoor clothes line holding several stiff towels, and shelves storing an array of paint cans, quart cans of automotive oil, and assorted supplies for Otto's car, including jumper cables.

There was a deep, concrete splash sink and faucet centered under the dust-encrusted window. Several old paint brushes which had been cleaned in gasoline lay on the tray at the side of the sink. A very basic work bench was pushed up against the wall next to the sink. A collection of well-worn tools hung from a peg board attached to the wall above the bench.

Charlie took all this in with a practiced look and dismissed it. He headed for a closed door to the right at the bottom of the stairs. He tried a switch to the left of the door and a small light bulb next to it lit up in red. He opened the door, stepping into a room bathed in a deep red light. He had found Otto's dark room.

A dozen photographs hung from a wire spanning the width of the room. They had not been pressed and were slightly curled and bowed, but it was easy to make out the subject matter. The pictures featured Shannon's current mayor pulling up yard signs of his opponent and stuffing the signs in the trunk of his car. There was no mistaking Alan Baker or what he was doing. Tampering with political yard signs was a hot button in Shannon; if these pictures wound up in the local newspaper it would be the end of his political career, for sure.

"That's probably worth fifty bucks a month to keep his position as mayor," Charlie said, thinking of Otto's going rates for small-town blackmail.

An old oak file cabinet in the corner drew Charlie's attention. It was one of the two-drawer affairs perched on top of a trestle-board table. Charlie opened the top drawer. The cabinet contained about a dozen folders of photographs with labels that were the names of Shannon-ites. Among them were Homer Schmidt, Doc Steiner, and Travis Hunt.

Homer's folder contained a single sheet of paper with hand-written notes pertaining to the offering at the Methodist Church, as well as a brief summary at the bottom of the page indicating how much Homer was to pay a month and when.

Doc Steiner's folder had a similar single sheet of paper with notes, but it also contained two small glass vials in a plastic bag that had, presumably, contained morphine for Otto's mother.

Charlie cringed at the thought of Otto's cold bloodedness in keeping them.

The folder for Travis Hunt held photographs of the love letters Blanche had mentioned, as well as several pictures taken at Blanche's house showing her and Travis embracing. Otto had obviously taken the photos while peeking in the dining room window off Blanche's car port.

'What a devil you were, Otto,' Charlie thought, reflecting on the dead man's brazen intrusion into the lives of his neighbors.

He dug into the file cabinet again, flipping through folders of other Shannon-ites who had fallen prey to Otto's skullduggery over the years. It was a chronology of human weaknesses and character flaws ranging from adultery to watermelon theft and everything in between. And Otto had profited handsomely from his opportunities. He and his camera had captured his fellow citizens in their moments of error, time-frozen and vulnerable to his demands. Charlie wondered when Otto found time to work at the post office.

*****

Chapter Forty-One

After finishing up at Otto's Charlie headed back uptown in the direction of his office. Charlie had just crossed over to the other side of Main Street when a car horn caught his attention. He turned to see who had honked, squinting into the bright sunlight, but his thoughts were diverted by Jo Dale heading his way. A big feller. With a limp.

"Well, damn," Charlie said to himself.

Jo Dale ambled up to where Charlie stood, a slight smile on his benign face.

"'Lo, Mr. Police Chief," Jo Dale said.

"Afternoon, Jo Dale," Charlie returned. The two men stood in front of the bakery. Charlie's mind swam with myriad thoughts: a gentle-spirited foundling, Margaret Cully's youngest boy, soap powder, berry picking … it couldn't be … a rusted bale hook protruding from Otto Hilty's eye. A big feller. With a limp.

Jo Dale was at ease, rocking on his feet, smiling contentedly. His one thought was just standing there in the sunshine.

Charlie tried to be gentle. "Jo Dale, you know anything about Otto Hilty getting killed in the livery barn?"

The big Indian shook his head, soberly.

"Were you anywhere near the livery barn the night Otto was killed?"

Jo Dale hung his head. After what seemed ages, he looked Charlie in the eye and gave a short nod.

A sinking feeling crept over Charlie; he dreaded what came next.

"Jo Dale, did you have anything to do with what happened to Otto in the barn?"

Jo Dale's eye grew big, but his face remained placid. It was his version of alarm. He shook his massive head.

Charlie made a decision, albeit a poor one.

"Look, Jo Dale," he said. "I need for you to come with me to my office where we can talk." He looked at the mountain of a man before him. Jo Dale easily made two of Charlie. One blow from his massive fist could kill a man.

"Turn around, Jo Dale," he said. "And put your hands behind your back." The gentle giant did as he was told, and Charlie slipped the handcuffs around Jo Dale's wrists. The cuffs cut into Jo Dale's flesh and he started to whimper. A large, solitary tear wedged out of his left eye and crawled down his cheek. More tears followed. Pretty soon, Jo Dale was blubbering pitifully, head hung down, his shoulders shaking in sadness and shame.

'Oh, Lord,' Charlie thought. 'What have I done?' "Let's go, Jo Dale," he said, taking hold of his arm and propelling him down the sidewalk.

They passed several people as they made their way to the police department. The citizens of Shannon stopped to stare, falling back as they passed. Some people voiced their shock, others their disapproval.

"What the hell you think you're doin', Charlie?"

"My God, Charlie! Jo Dale wouldn't hurt a fly!"

"Look, Jo Dale's bleedin' from those handcuffs!"

"This is wrong, Simmons! Just plain wrong!"

"Don't you worry none, Jo Dale! This is all a mistake!"

By the time Charlie rounded the corner at the town hall heading for his office there was a crowd of at least twenty people following him and Jo Dale. One man carried a hand-written sign that read, 'Free our Injun.' Charlie stopped and turned to face the throng of concerned citizens.

"Go on home, folks," Charlie told them.

"Let him go, Charlie!"

"You go on home!"

"Picking on a man can't defend himself!"

"He shoulda been locked up years ago!"

At this last utterance, the crowd gasped. Everyone looked wildly about, trying to figure out who had said this last despicable thing, but whoever had said it realized his faux pas and kept still.

"Enough!" Charlie roared. "I need to talk to Jo Dale and that's just what I'm a gonna do. Now, you all go on home!" He sent

Jo Dale through the door to the jail and followed immediately after, closing, and locking the door.

"Now, Jo Dale," Charlie said, "I'm goin' to remove those handcuffs, but you need to promise me you won't do anything crazy or try to get away." He waited for Jo Dale to speak, but the big man kept silent, his head hung and his shoulders slouched.

Charlie sighed. He felt worse than Jo Dale at what was happening. He unlocked the shackles and was chagrined that the metal had, indeed, cut into Jo Dale's wrists. He put in a call to Doc Steiner and asked him to pay a house call at the jail, then he herded his prisoner into a cell, made sure he had a blanket and pillow, and closed the cell door without locking it. Through it all, Jo Dale had not said a single word.

Several minutes later there was a knock at the office door. It was his wife, Faerie. Surprised, he opened the door. Faerie never came to the police department when he was working there. She bustled in, carrying a basket covered with a white linen cloth.

"What brings you here, wife?" Charlie asked.

She whirled on him, mad as a spitting cat.

"Charlie Simmons," she began, "I'm just thankful your dear mama isn't here to see this shameful thing you've done today."

"Wha …"

"I never thought I'd live to see the day you became such a cruel, unthinking human being," she said, her voice edging toward shrillness. "What on *earth* were you thinking, shackling poor Jo Dale in public and parading him down the street like some sort of circus exhibit? *Our* Jo Dale, Charlie. We've known him all our lives. Grown up with him. How could you do this to him, Charlie? How?"

Charlie was unable to think of a response and was saved from doing so by another knock on the door. It was Doc Steiner.

"Charlie," Doc said, trying to sound forbearing. He had heard about the ruckus from half a dozen town folk and was none too pleased with their version of what had transpired earlier with Jo Dale being paraded through town to the jail. The frown on his mouth stretched clear to his forehead and his manner was uncharacteristically stiff toward Charlie.

"Afternoon, Faerie," he said when he stepped into the office.

"Hello, Doc," she replied. She was visibly upset, he could see.

"What am I doing here, Charlie?" he asked.

Charlie nodded toward the cell housing Jo Dale. "I need you to take a look at Jo Dale's wrists, Doc," he said.

"What's wrong with his wrists?" Doc asked. He knew full well, since he heard the scuttlebutt about it all on the street, but he wanted to hear Charlie say it.

Charlie cleared his voice. "The handcuffs were a little tight," he said. An awkward silence ensued. "His cell's unlocked," he added, motioning with his head.

Doc entered Jo Dale's cell and bent to examine the cuts on the big man's wrists. He swore under his breath at what he saw. He gently cleaned and dressed the wounds, speaking to his patient in soothing tones all the while. Like everyone else in Shannon, Doc treated Jo Dale like a large child. When he had finished his doctoring, he patted Jo Dale reassuringly on the shoulder and exited the cell.

"Everything OK, Doc?" Charlie asked.

"The cuts on his wrists will heal," Doc replied. Doc headed toward the door to leave, carrying his medical bag. "As to the rest, we'll see," he said, and he left.

Charlie wasn't sure what Doc's parting words referred to, and they made him feel apprehensive. He felt like he had opened Pandora's box and loosed more trouble than he could fathom.

Faerie entered Jo Dale's cell with her basket and proceeded to spread the food she had brought him on his bunk.

"I hope you like mincemeat pie, Jo Dale," she said, busying herself with plates and silverware. "And there's hot coffee or cider to drink."

In the small cell the scent of laundry detergent from Jo Dale's clothes was almost over-powering. It was mitigated by a faint sour smell brought on by the stress of his situation. Faerie stopped her monologue to glance at Jo Dale. With his wrists in bandages and his face swollen from crying he was a sorry sight.

"Why you poor thing," Faerie soothed. "Do you want I should get you …"

"That will do, Faerie," Charlie interrupted. "He doesn't need coddling. He's my prisoner, for Pete's sake."

Faerie had been an only child, but not from a wealthy family. Her mother had taken sick after giving birth to Faerie and never really recovered her strength, so when she was old enough Faerie took over running the house for her mom, dad, and herself.

She and Charlie never had any kids. For whatever reason, they could not have children so Faerie satisfied her maternal urges by teaching Sunday school and helping less fortunate people, the Jo Dales of Shannon, in need.

She had a sweet disposition and the dimples to prove it. When she smiled her face was prettily jolly, accentuated by a classic divot in the cleft of her chin, which was frequent because Faerie did an awful lot of smiling. Charlie often reflected that his wife's good nature radiated out from within, making life in her sphere a blessing for those who shared it.

Make no mistake: Faerie Simmons was not a woman who suffered fools lightly. She had a temper that flashed and burned, but quickly died down, again.

"You can be positively loathsome sometimes, Charlie Simmons! Don't expect a warm dinner from me tonight!" She gave a last reassuring look at Jo Dale, a dark scowl at her husband, and stormed out the door. Even Lion had turned his back on his master and was holed up in Jo Dale's cell, curled into a ball and asleep on the end of Jo Dale's cot.

Charlie sighed. He was not used to being the bad guy, but if Jo Dale was responsible for Otto's murder he needed to be locked up. That was the law. He walked over to Jo Dale's cell; the big man looked lost and dejected.

"Jo Dale," Charlie said, but got no response.

He tried again. "Look at me, Jo Dale," Charlie said.

The prisoner swung his enormous, smooth-skinned face toward Charlie.

"I need to ask you some questions about the night Otto Hilty was killed," Charlie said. "I'm not accusing you of anything, Jo Dale, but I just want you to tell me what you know, OK?"

There was no response from Jo Dale. He sat on his bunk like a mountain and didn't move a muscle or show any emotion in his face. He merely waited.

"Were you at the old livery barn behind the Presbyterian Church the Saturday night of Harvest Festival weekend, Jo Dale?" Charlie asked.

The big Indian said nothing.

"Did you see Otto Hilty at the barn?"

Nothing.

Charlie was getting frustrated at Jo Dale's silence. He took a slow breath before continuing; it was an effort to keep his voice calm.

"Jo Dale, did you see who killed Otto that night?"

Charlie's words tripped the start button in Jo Dale's brain and the horror movie started to play across the screen in his mind. Otto Hilty lying on the straw of the barn floor with a bail hook plunged into his eye. He looked like a giant trout, with his mouth opening and closing like a fish when it's caught and lifted out of the water. Otto staring at him with his one good eye, until the light of life finally went from it and his mouth stopped moving.

The memory of what he saw caused Jo Dale to tremble all over, and he emitted a mournful keening sound as he rocked back and forth on his bunk. The smell of fear mingled with the scent of the laundry soap infused in his clothing.

"Jo Dale, did you kill Otto?" Charlie asked in barely a whisper.

*****

Chapter Forty-Two

Early the next morning Doc Steiner banged open the door to Charlie's office with his medical bag, which he plopped in the chair opposite the desk from where Charlie sat.

"Mornin', Doc," Charlie offered. He was on his second cup of coffee after spending the night watching over his prisoner to make sure he wouldn't harm himself.

Doc huffed back. He entered the cell where Jo Dale was sitting on his narrow bed to check his bandaged wrists. Satisfied there was no danger of infection, he changed the bandages. He spoke in low, soothing tones to Jo Dale as he had the day before, anything to try and ease the fear and dejection the gentle giant must be feeling. When he was finished with his doctoring, he left Jo Dale and took the chair opposite Charlie's.

"Want some coffee, Doc?"

Doc's look said 'no.' "No, Charlie, I sure as hell don't want any coffee. What I want is for you to let Jo Dale go home."

"Now, Doc," Charlie began.

Doc held up his right hand to block Charlie's words. "No, you listen to me, Charlie Simmons," he said. "There's no way in hell Jo Dale killed Otto Hilty."

"But Doc, I questioned Jo Dale last night and he all but admitted to killing Otto," Charlie said.

Doc's mouth dropped open.

"Jo Dale said he killed Otto?" he asked, in disbelief.

Charlie squirmed. "Well, not in so many words, but …"

"No, sir," Doc interrupted. "No, I can't believe it."

Charlie set his coffee mug on his desk. He knew Doc well enough to see what was coming next. He resigned himself to listen to whatever story Doc concocted about Jo Dale's innocence.

"Why do you say that, Doc?" he asked.

Doc took a deep breath. "Because, Charlie," he said, "I went through Old Doc Travers' records last night and pulled his records for Jo Dale."

Doctor Travers had been the town's doctor long before Doc Steiner took over as Shannon's doctor in residence after his retirement.

"And?" Charlie said.

"And according to Doc's records Jo Dale had a procedure done on him when he was a little boy. A procedure that would have made it virtually impossible for him to do something as violent as what was done to Otto Hilty."

Doc had Charlie's attention. He sensed a *coup de grâce* coming.

"Jo Dale was castrated as a young boy, Charlie."

"Which means …?" Charlie asked.

196

"Why, it's suspected that castration makes aggressive behavior almost impossible."

Charlie thought about Doc's statement for a minute. "So," he said, "you're saying Jo Dale is incapable of being aggressive and therefore did not kill Otto? And it's not based on actual fact, but a suspicion?"

"Well, er …" Doc stumbled.

"Doc, that's less conclusive than the evidence I got that says Jo Dale did kill Otto."

Doc had been watching Jo Dale nibbling at a hot-cross-bun Miss Faerie had left for his breakfast. He suddenly jumped out of his seat.

"That's it!" Doc cried, excited. He turned to face Charlie, triumph written across his face.

Now it was Charlie's turn to be flummoxed. "What's it, Doc?"

Doc hurriedly poured a cup of steaming coffee and carried it to Jo Dale's cell.

"Here, son," he said. "Try some of this coffee with that roll." He put the cup of coffee in Jo Dale's right hand. Jo Dale seemed confused for a minute, then transferred the mug to his left hand before sipping the hot liquid. He set the cup down and resumed eating.

"Take another sip, Jo Dale," Doc said, putting the cup in the Indian's big right paw. Again, Jo Dale put the cup in his other hand before taking a drink.

"There! Ya see!" Doc said, jubilantly. "He couldn't have killed Otto Hilty!"

The light went on in Charlie's brain, finally, and he saw that Doc was right. Whoever had killed Otto had been a right-handed person. Clearly, Jo Dale was a southpaw.

Charlie had no choice but to release Jo Dale. Doc insisted Jo Dale be admitted to the hospital in Shannon for a few days for observation, just to make sure there was no danger he would try and harm himself from all the stress and fear Charlie had put him through.

"And the town can pick up the tab for the hospital bill, and mine, too," Doc huffed.

Jo Dale was not used to being so fussed over, but he went docilely with Doc, hoping there was some cherry pie somewhere at the end of it all.

*****

Chapter Forty-Three

Saturday dawned bright and crisp, a perfect autumn day in northwest Ohio. The air had that slightly moldy smell from fallen leaves, and a nutty scent from the black walnut and butternut trees that grew in the surrounding woodlands.

The local cider mill was in full production, and a steady stream of customers made their way to the little red barn that housed the mill on the Russell Diller farm that sat at the northeast edge of town. They brought gallon and half-gallon glass jugs to be filled under the tap of the massive cider keg Russell continuously refilled with fresh pressings. Apple fritters, cinnamon doughnuts, Indian corn, and a variety of gourds were also for sale.

Charlie had filled a jug of the tangy brew and stood chatting with Russell.

"Quite a nice little business you got goin' here, Russ," he said.

Russell's face beamed with pride. "Best cider around," he said. "Don't use no ground apples in my juice."

Russell was referring to the fact that many cider producers juiced apples that were picked up from the ground. These ground apples were often wormy or partially rotted but were thrown into the presser along with apples picked from the tree.

"You have a good crop this year?" Charlie asked, just making conversation.

"Praise God, we did!" Russell replied. "A real bounty. I always especially appreciate a bumper crop in anything, after what we went through with rationing in the war. 'Course, those of us livin' on a farm didn't feel the pinch near like what you town folks felt."

Charlie nodded. He well remembered the shortages during WWII. One of the first things to be rationed, he remembered, had been sugar. His brother, Cliff, had seen shortages coming, and had stockpiled more than several hundred pounds of sugar at home before the rationing had actually begun. He had stacked it all on his kitchen table and wedged boxes underneath the table to support it.

When Cliff had gone to the schoolhouse to register for his ration stamps and been asked how much sugar he had at home, he had replied, "Just what's on my kitchen table."

"Well, that can't be more than a couple of pounds," the ration's clerk replied, stamping Cliff's card and issuing him his coupons.

Women's silk hose had also been scarce. Cars were at a premium, and the dealers often stored what automobiles they had in warehouses, out of sight. They doled the cars out to the highest bidder, and to those with jobs that benefited the country and required a car. Meat was rationed, too, and farmers butchered their livestock and sold the meat on the growing black market. Butter, fish, cigarettes, and cheese had become scarce, and ration stamps had been needed to buy a pair of shoes.

Even though Charlie owned a farm, he had turned his farm over to his brother, John, to manage. Charlie had never really liked working the land, and he and Faerie had never had any children to help with the farm work, so he had enlisted John to do the work and they split the profits. Charlie had moved back into town and worked in his brother's garage, as well as standing in for the police chief when Pete Gaite was out of town. He had been able to rely on what his and his brothers' farms produced to help him and Faerie weather the rationing.

"Hope to never see nuthin' like that again in my lifetime," Russell was saying, referring to the war. "All them houses around town with their blue stars and gold stars … lost too many good people over there," he said.

Russell's mention of the blue and gold stars jogged something in Charlie's mind. He closed his eyes, straining to remember what it was, but like a winged butterfly the memory flitted just out of his reach. Then, he had it.

"A blue star meant there was a boy in service; a gold star meant 'killed in action'. We shot five volleys over Bertha Stalling's house … she sent five boys off to that damn war. I remember the picture the Shannon News ran of her five grown sons standing 'round her when they came back home."

Turley's words in the barber shop had suddenly come back to him. That was it! The picture that had been taken from Otto's house. It all clicked into place for Charlie in that instant.

"Thanks, Turley," he muttered to himself, as he headed back to his office. He now thought he knew who had killed Otto Hilty, and why. And it all went back to Katie Mohler.

Chapter Forty-Four

That night Charlie woke out of a sound sleep. He elbowed his Faerie in the side and told her, "I just found Katie Mohler."

"What are you talkin' about?" his wife asked.

"I just found her. She's all doubled up in a well."

"Aw, you're dreamin'," Faerie replied. "Go back to sleep."

The next morning was Sunday. Charlie figured out what he would need to find Katie Mohler. He went over to his brother's garage and cut a half-inch-in-diameter iron rod into a four-foot length. He bent five inches on one end of the rod into an L-shape, to give it a handle like a cane, and on the other end he ground a sharp point.

He went across the street to his neighbor's house, where Alby Brode lived, and knocked on the door.

"Alby," he said, when Alby came to the door, "let's go out to the Mohler farm this morning. I'm gonna find Katie Mohler."

Alby laughed, but said, "Well, I haven't got nuthin' else to do, Charlie. Sure, I'll go with you."

When they arrived at the Mohler farm there were a lot of people there, milling around, ostensibly hunting for Mrs. Mohler. It was around eleven o'clock.

"Most of these folks will go to lunch, shortly," Charlie said. "Let's meander down by the creek for a while until this crowd clears out. I want to look up next to the barn where that lean-to has been built onto the side of it."

They headed across a field of corn stubble toward the low end of the farm where a small creek ran through. Rolland Simmons caught sight of his uncle and came running toward him.

"What are you doin' out here, Uncle Charlie?" Rolland asked. "You think you're gonna find Mrs. Mohler and get that reward?" He fell in with his uncle and Alby and followed them around.

"Aren't you supposed to be home for lunch, Rolland?" Charlie asked, a bit peevishly. He wanted Rolland to quit tagging along; this was not the kind of thing a young man ought to see, he reasoned. But Rolland continued to dog the two men. When they got to the creek they ran into Clyde Gratz. Clyde's farm was just the other side of the creek. When Charlie told Clyde what he intended to do, Clyde decided to join them.

"Where you gonna look that's any different from where everybody else has already searched?" Rolland asked. "Every inch of this farm and his other farm on the north side of town has been gone over more 'n a dozen times."

"Years ago, when I was about your age, Rolland, I helped bail hay on this farm. At that time, there was an old well next to the barn. Mohler built a lean-to against the barn on that side and covered the well up, but it's still there, I'm certain. That's where I want to look."

The four men kicked around the creek bottom for a while, killing time. Just before noon, they started back toward the barn. By now, the crowd had thinned out, heading home for Sunday dinner. They arrived at the door of the lean-to.

Charlie turned to Rolland. "This might not be somethin' you should see, Rolland," he said. "Maybe you'd be better off headin' home for dinner, too."

Rolland stood firm. "I saw old Mrs. Hauenstein burned to a crisp on her kitchen floor," he told his uncle. "I can handle this."

Charlie pulled the door to the lean-to open. There was about two feet of space just inside the door, and then the lean-to was packed solid with standing shocks of corn. The men began moving the corn shocks out of the way to work their way to the other end of the lean-to, and pretty soon the door was blocked off by the shocks they'd moved.

They made a narrow path to the back of the lean-to, and Charlie used the sharpened tool he had fashioned to prod the earth in this area. After several attempts he found where the soil was less packed, almost soft, and he began to probe in this area. After a few prods, his iron rod went clear down.

The only light in the lean-to was the sunlight that filtered through the slatted sides of the structure. Visibility was low in the gloomy interior, and the dust stirred up from moving the corn shocks made seeing anything even more difficult.

On his next jab, Charlie got something caught on his probe. Clyde Gratz lit a match and held it up to see what it was. Rolland crowded in close to look. A mass at the end of the iron point looked to be a part of a woman's private part, surrounded by light brown pubic hair caked with dirt.

The shocked silence following this grim discovery was broken by Rolland letting out a high-pitched scream. Clyde had to blow the match out; his fingers were getting burned. The darkness made Rolland even more frantic.

"I need outta here!" Rolland said, panic rising in his voice with each word he spoke. "Outta here! Outta here!" He started going to pieces.

"Now Rolland," Charlie said, trying to calm the young man. "I'm goin' to get you outta here just as soon as I can, but we've got to make a way by movin' this corn again."

The three men set to work moving the corn shocks to the back so they could make a path back to the door of the lean-to. When they were almost finished, Charlie cautioned his nephew.

"Now, Rolland," he said, "I don't want you to tell anybody what we found here, understand? If word got out about this some folks in town might try and take the law into their own hands and hurt old man Mohler, so don't say anything, OK?" He was afraid a lynching mob would be the end of Hiram Mohler before he could be turned over to the authorities.

Rolland nodded, his eyes wide as an owl's.

Charlie moved the last of the corn shocks out of the way and opened the door of the lean-to, but before he could stand aside, Rolland had crawled through Charlie's legs and bolted out the door. He made it about ten feet and retched, reliving

the horror of what he had seen. Then, wiping his face with his
sleeve, he lit out for his dad's house.

Rolland did not stop running until he reached the safety of the
house on Elm Street. He burst into the dining room, trying to
catch his breath. His stepmom, dad, sister, and younger
brothers had just sat down to Sunday dinner and looked up in
alarm when he rushed in.

"Why, Rolland," his father, Cliff, said, "What on earth's the
matter? Where have you been?"

Rolland was bent over, panting. "I daresn't tell, I daresn't tell,"
he gasped.

"You daresn't tell what, Son?" Cliff asked. "Why are you so out
of breath? Where were you?"

Rolland had to tell someone. "Mohler's farm," he gasped.
"With Charlie. He found Katie Mohler all chopped up in pieces
in an old well and my gawd, it was somethin' awful!"

*****

Chapter Forty-Five

Just after Rolland ran off Hiram Mohler returned to his farm from town. He parked his truck by the back door of his farmhouse and began walking over towards the barn where Charlie, Alby, and Clyde stood. He had a lopsided grin on his face as he approached, and when he saw the door open to the lean-to the grin disappeared, replaced by a wild leer. He stopped.

Charlie stepped forward. "Hiram, you need to come with me," he said.

Hiram looked from Charlie to Alby, and then to Clyde. A look of pure loathing flashed on his face.

"You're the reason I done it, Gratz," he spat. "You and that fool brother of yours."

"Did what, Hiram?" Charlie asked.

Hiram's gaze swung back to where Charlie stood. "Why, killed Otto Hilty, a course," he said matter-of-factly.

"You killed Otto?" Charlie asked.

Hiram broke into a raucous cackle. "I sure did," he said, almost proudly. "Hooked 'im in the eye with that bail hook, I did." He tee-heed. "Just like hooking a big fish," he added. "Ya shoulda seen him floppin' around." Hiram enjoyed remembering the event; the others grimaced at the monstrosity before them.

"Why is you killin' Otto my fault …" Clyde began, but Charlie held up his hand to silence him.

Hiram stood, solemnly nodding his head before he answered Clyde. "It's all on account of me burnin' you and Tom's barns," he said, as if that explained it all.

"Hiram, are you confessing to burnin' both the Gratz brothers' barns?" Charlie asked.

Clyde clenched his fists and took a step in Hiram's direction. "You crazy old bast …" he began, before Charlie intercepted him.

"I am," Hiram said. He was mighty pleased with himself. "I told you and Tom I'd be back and that you'd be sorry for crossing me," he went on.

"What about Katie?" Charlie asked.

Hiram's face went through a series of expressions, beginning with profound grief. "My wife, may God rest her soul, was a good woman." He nodded several times, reassuring himself of her worth. Anger suddenly clouded his visage. "But she stuck her nose in where it didn't belong, didn't she? That was her undoing. Busybody! She just wouldn't let it go."

"Let what go, Hiram?" Charlie pressed.

The old farmer gestured widely with his arm in the direction of the Gratz brothers' properties. "Them barns I burned," he replied. "She come back from town one day in a stew about people in Shannon thinkin' I burned the barns, so I decided to burn mine, too, so's to divert suspicion. She followed me out to the barn to try and stop me, and that's when I had to kill her." He said it with such calm it made the other men gasp in disgust.

"Good Lord!" Alby exclaimed, involuntarily.

"You're insane," Clyde Gratz murmured.

Hiram just stood there, a vile leer now in possession of his face.

"And did you also have to chop her up like a butchered hog?" Charlie asked, his voice still and cold.

Hiram looked down at his feet, then back up at Charlie. "Well, now," he began, but he couldn't go any further. His eyes dropped, but only for a moment. "Katie had no call interferin' in my business," he said defiantly. "She should a just minded the house and kept still."

"Why Otto, Hiram? What had he done?" Charlie wanted to know.

"Katie was bound to say something to Otto 'bout the barns," he said. "He was the one person she woulda told. I couldn't take the chance a Otto trying to blackmail me like he did others in town."

There was a pause while the three men processed what Hiram had said. Alby finally had to turn away; he couldn't stomach what was happening.

"Katie was your wife, you sick bastard," Clyde said. "She was the only good thing about you."

Hiram looked downcast, briefly. When he glanced at Clyde, he had a sly look about him. "You sniffin' 'round my Katie, Gratz?" he teased.

"Why, you nasty old cur!" Clyde roared, lunging for Hiram.

Charlie threw himself between the two men, averting a brawl. "Enough!" he commanded. "You, Hiram, just shut your mouth!" Charlie ordered.

Hiram looked pleased with himself, then adopted an air of contrition. He allowed Charlie to handcuff him and load him into the back of his car. Charlie had Alby Brode climb in the back to keep Hiram in line, then drove them back to Shannon.

Word had already spread, by way of Rolland, that Katie Mohler's remains had been found in a well on Hiram's farm where he had chopped her up and buried her. When Charlie arrived at the police department with his prisoner, even though it was Sunday, a crowd of townspeople had gathered outside the department.

When Charlie pulled Hiram out of the rear seat the gathering crowded in close to the car. The murmurings of the group escalated in volume until one onlooker finally shouted, "Hang 'im!"

This outburst was followed by total silence, but only briefly. Somebody else pitched in, "We don't allow wife murderers in our town!"

"Someone get a rope!"

"Take him behind the church to that oak tree!"

"Let's settle this now!"

The chorus of voices was growing angrier by the minute. Charlie feared he was facing a lynch mob, so he did the only thing he knew to do. He shoved Hiram back into the rear of his car, got behind the wheel, locked the car doors, and drove him to the county jail in Lima. There, at least, no one knew him, and the county had the proper authorities to protect him, even though Charlie privately thought a noose might save the town and taxpayers the trouble and expense of a trial and the sentence that would follow.

*****

Hiram languished in the Allen county jail for two months while the authorities considered their options available for prosecuting him. Life in jail was easy for Hiram. He got fed three squares a day, his clothes were provided, and he had a cell all to himself. He was a model prisoner, except for the fact that he had heinously killed two people in cold blood and showed not the slightest remorse for his actions. The DA's office wanted to convict him and send him to death row, but the public defender found three different doctors who claimed Hiram was certifiable and unable to stand trial since he was mad as a hatter.

Hiram sat in on the deliberations with a keen look on his face, following the debate over his fate. The PDA's office wanted to see Hiram fry; the Public Defender's office sought to confine him to a mental institution. Back and forth they went.

Hiram finally cleared his throat and announced, "Katie was dead afore I chopped her into bits." Everyone stared at him in surprise. Hiram suddenly appeared shy, ducking his head coyly. "Does that help any?" he asked.

There was a stunned silence followed by the public defender saying, "I rest my case."

Hiram was transferred to the Lima Correctional Institute for the Criminally Insane to live out his days.

*****

Chapter Forty-Six

"They say there's ghosts all over the place, Charlie," Rolland said in a half-whisper. "Cell doors openin' and closin' all by themselves, lights turnin' on and off, footsteps echoin' in empty hallways and common areas. Why, there's even a phantom figure dressed in black they see passin' right through the steel doors, movin' from cell to cell. And some female apparition named Mary that moans and screams 'Help me, help me.' The guards run up to the second floor to see what's goin' on and nobody's there."

Rolland's high school health class had gone to the Lima Correctional Institute for the Criminally Insane on a field trip earlier in the day and the experience had unnerved Rolland to the point that it was all he could talk about. Wide-eyed, his words came in a rush.

"I swear, Uncle Charlie, I ain't never seen nuthin' like it before in my whole life."

Charlie thought somebody up at the high school had a screw loose to expose young people to something as horrific as the nut house in nearby Lima. He shook his head at the shear lunacy. He had been to the hospital once in his life, when he was a good ten years older than Rolland, and that had been enough for him. Even now, listening to Rolland, it gave him the creeps to think about what he had seen on his visit.

Opened in 1915, the Lima State Hospital was the second largest poured concrete structure in the world, after the

Pentagon. The structure had a steel-reinforced framework driven to the bedrock underneath it, and the walls were fourteen inches thick. It was the Titanic of buildings, designed to be impregnable.

It had the distinction of being the largest institution for the criminally insane, a hulking complex of buildings that took in the most violent, crazed criminals from all over the country. It warehoused the worst of the worst. Primates who had traveled beyond the perimeters of humanity and were in freefall in the uncharted dimension of psychological terror, their minds unraveling like a ball of string batted to and fro by a playful kitten.

Some inmates ran around stark naked because the hospital staff could not keep clothes on them. On his visit, Charlie had seen through a slot in a shower room door where one woman was locked up day and night because it was easier to clean her messes up in the tiled room. And then there was Ward 21, where inmates were forced to sit on hard wooden chairs all day without moving or speaking.

It was a dark and dangerous place for the people who were incarcerated there, as well as for those who worked there. Abuse of the inmates was legendary and sadistic. The medical care was deplorable. It was not uncommon for an inmate to check into the infirmary and never get back out alive, such was the reputation of the sadistic doctor who ran it.

It was rumored that frontal lobotomies were routinely performed here using primitive tools by an untrained staff, leaving the inmates victimized by the procedure permanently and wretchedly in vegetative states or mercifully dead.

The other major scandal associated with the medical clinic was that it performed forced abortions on female inmates impregnated by the hospital guards who sexually assaulted the women they were supposed to be supervising and protecting. The hospital was a place of horror beyond anything imaginable.

Inmates managed to escape periodically, sending the residents within a ten-mile radius into a panic. When the escape siren sounded, reverberating over the massive loudspeakers planted around the facility's perimeter, it struck terror to the general population. Even people in Shannon went on the alert, and farm wives kept a rifle handy.

"Isn't Lima where Crazy Mohler ended up?" Rolland asked his uncle in a whisper.

Charlie nodded. "It is, Rolland," he answered.

Rolland's eyes widened even more. "Think of that," he mused. "I mighta walked right past his cell and not even known," he said.

"I'm pretty sure Hiram was nowhere near your class," Charlie said. "Somebody that dangerous would be locked up deep within the bowels of that place. Probably never see the light of day."

*****

Chapter Forty-Seven

Hiram Mohler's first month at the Lima Correctional facility was spent in solitary confinement. This was the usual procedure for an inmate with such a violent criminal history. Solitary suited Hiram just fine, but it was a relief when he was introduced into a more mainstream environment. He still pretty much kept to himself but was curious about his fellow inmates and entertained by their activities.

The hospital segregated the men from the women and the animals from the savages. The animals were, in Hiram's mind, those inmates who would not keep their clothes on or who defecated on themselves or others. The savages were the wild men who ruled by intimidation and brutality. Hiram considered himself a savage, though he was not into dominating his neighbors. He just wanted to be left alone. Compared to some of his fellow inmates, Hiram seemed almost sane.

After a three-month trial period without incident Hiram was given permission to spend two afternoons a week in the large shop on the hospital premises. The shop was supposed to be a privilege for the inmates with no or relatively few behavior problems and was considered a major part of the hospital's rehabilitation program. That was a joke: there was nothing rehabilitative about Lima's nut house. The shop was also where the prisoners made license plates for the state to sell.

Hiram was watching the license plate assembly process one afternoon. He was almost mesmerized by the large stamping machine that stamped the raised numbers and letters on the tin plates. The big black man running the machine, Blue, had a rhythm to his work and Hiram was fascinated by how quickly and musically the man operated the huge piece of equipment.

Seemingly out of nowhere, another inmate approached the stamping machine operator and started to harass him, calling him names and slurring his work. The verbal assault soon interfered with the stamper's work and his rhythm was broken by the harangue. His whole process finally shut down, and he narrowly missed getting one of his hands mangled by the industrial machine. The tirade continued.

Hiram had really been enjoying himself as he watched the stamping process. When the heckler would not shut up and let Blue get on with his work Hiram picked up a hammer and bludgeoned him to death, then motioned with the dripping hammer for Blue to continue. Blue eyed Hiram, wondering if he would be next, but Hiram put the hammer aside and smiled at him to get on with his work.

"Thanks, man," Blue muttered, trying to get his groove back.

The guards in the tool shop finally noticed the dead inmate. Blue said nothing, just kept on stamping. Hiram confessed readily to his crime.

"Perfectly defensible," he told the guards, serenely. "The man was interfering with Blue, here."

The guards did not share Hiram's point of view. He was shackled and led off to solitary confinement. When the steel door clanged shut Hiram suddenly realized he was not seen as a hero for getting Blue's production back online; he was being punished.

"Wait!" he yelled after the retreating guards. "Let me outta here! There's one more I got to kill!"

*****

Chapter Forty-Eight

Wesley Montgomery lived alone about a mile and a half from the city limits of Shannon on the town's northwestern edge off County Line Road. His wife, Erma, had died years earlier and he had stayed on the farm. It was the only home he had ever known. Wesley had been born on this same farm and taken it over when his parents were killed in a car accident involving a semi-truck on State Route 30.

In his late fifties, Wesley didn't keep much livestock any more other than a few chickens and sheep he liked to see in pasture under the fruit trees in the old orchard beside the farmhouse. He leased the land out for planting to one of his neighbors and, for all intents and purposes, Wesley was retired.

He was also a tired man. An accident with a corn picker had left him lame in his left leg, with limited use of his left arm. He got around without a cane, but dragged that left leg of his a bit when he walked. Wesley made do, was able to cook for himself after a fashion, but the old farmhouse had not had a good cleaning since Emma's passing. It smelled of old grease, liniment, and lack of care.

The linoleum on the farm kitchen's floor had yellowed with age and layers of wax, and it was cracked and breaking in the heavily worn areas in front of the sink and refrigerator. The Formica- topped table had the same disease. The ruffled curtains at the windows were stiff with grime. The kitchen would never again smell of fresh-baked rolls, apple pie, or savory roast. It was pretty damn depressing.

This late April morning the daylight had not fully overcome night's darkness. The air had a slight chill, and a damp fog swirled over the lawn in the weak light from the lamp post at the end of the sidewalk leading from the back door toward the barn and shop.

Wesley woke with a start. The recurring nightmare had left him in a cold sweat, even in his flannel pajamas. Always the same. Hiram Mohler had come to make good on his threat to kill him.

Word was spreading around Shannon that Hiram had taken a hammer to one of his fellow inmate's head in the shop in the insane asylum. He had killed him dead as a door nail. The prison guards had subdued and shackled Hiram and, as they led him off to solitary Hiram had struggled to break free.

"Let me outta here!" he had shouted. "There's one more I got to kill!"

That one more was Wesley Montgomery. He and Hiram had had words on more than one occasion through the years, primarily over who was entitled to pick the spongey-topped morel mushrooms when they popped up through the humus and layers of fallen and decaying leaves in Wes' woods and orchard. Wesley's woods had a high concentration of ash and elm trees which supported the delicate mushroom's growth. Beneath the cherry and apple trees in the orchard were habitats attractive to the morel spores, as well.

Hiram had a small farm that adjoined Wesley's farm, and several times Wes had caught Hiram picking his morels. Wesley could never get his mind around Hiram's attitude toward his mushrooms. Like that should even be an issue, right? It was Wesley's land, but for some twisted reason Hiram thought he had the rights to Wesley's morels.

The war of words escalated over time and finally erupted into an all-out fist fight, with Wesley the victor. This was before his run-in with the corn picker when he could handle his own. More than Hiram's pride was wounded, and he promised Wesley he would kill him some day. Everybody in town knew it.

The false sense of security Wesley felt from Hiram's being locked up was just that: false. There wasn't a day went by he didn't cringe at Hiram's threat. He lived looking behind his back and told his neighbors and friends to always call out when they came to visit to let him know who was there. Wesley was jumpy. He kept a loaded rifle next to the kitchen door, and he slept with a loaded revolver under his pillow. He would not be taken easily.

Wesley pushed the covers aside and swung his legs over the edge of the bed, feeling for the worn felt slippers with his gnarled feet. He sighed. Rolland Simmons was stopping by this morning with a load of chicken feed and Wesley wanted to supervise where he unloaded it. He dressed, splashed cold water on his grizzled face, and shuffled out to the kitchen.

With the coffee percolating Wes turned to preparing his every-morning breakfast: two eggs, sunny-side, with toast. The old cast-iron skillet perched perpetually on the back burner was so seasoned his eggs never stuck, and it didn't need to be washed. It sat there, year after year, awaiting his two morning eggs.

This morning he paused a moment, thinking of his Erma. She had been the one who had seasoned the skillet, coating it inside and out with a film of lard, then baking it in the oven. She had repeated the process two more times because she went by the maxim that once was never enough. Dear God, how he missed her!

With breakfast over and the washing up done, Wesley spent time on his daily devotions. By the time he had finished, day had officially arrived with an anemic squawk from his lazy rooster, Gideon. A slight rap at the kitchen door was followed by an aggressive pounding, and he rose to greet his caller.

He opened the door to find Rolland Simmons standing on this stoop.

"Mornin', Rolland," he said.

Rolland uttered a strangled response. Puzzled, Wesley searched Rolland's face. Rolland's eyes were wide with terror, and his features were contorted to such an extent he did not look like himself.

"Why, Rolland …" Wesley began.

Rolland was suddenly thrown off to one side like a rag doll and in his place stood Hiram Mohler, a look of pure delighted hatred gleaming from his eyes.

Wesley's eyes bulged in terror, and his stomach lurched. For an instant, Wesley thought he was back in his nightmare. Hiram disavowed him of that theory when he crashed against the door, throwing Wesley backwards into the kitchen, where he banged into one of the vinyl-backed kitchen chairs.

He grabbed hold of the countertop to steady himself. Too late, he saw his ever-ready rifle leaning in the corner near the door jamb. There was no way he could get past Mohler to reach the weapon.

Wesley's thoughts raced in multiple directions as he sought a way to defend himself against his mad nemesis. When he looked at Hiram his bowels almost let go at what he saw. Hiram's right hand, raised above his head ready to strike, held a hatchet. Its honed edge gleamed faintly as the weak light from the kitchen ceiling bulb caught its sheen.

"I been waitin' for this day to come for a long, long time, Montgomery," Hiram hooted. He shook the hatchet menacingly. "And I just spent a half hour in your shop sharpening your hatchet 'til it could splice a hair." He leered, pleased with himself. "And now I'm a gonna do to you what I did to my Katie."

*****

Chapter Forty-Nine

Rolland ran like the wind after Hiram shoved him aside at Wesley's back door. He completely forgot he had driven the delivery truck to Wesley's farm and lit out running for Shannon. He felt like he was flying, and perhaps he was. As a young boy Rolland often imagined going airborne as he ran, being suddenly lifted aloft, and he had that sensation now as he thundered down County Line Road in the direction of town.

As he ran, he replayed the scene that had unfolded shortly after his arrival at the Montgomery farm. Crazy Man Mohler had been hiding behind the enormous blooming forsythia bush that grew up against the back of Wesley's house to the right of the kitchen door.

When Rolland reached to knock on the door, as he had always been instructed to do to alert Wesley of his presence, Mohler sprang out of the bushes wielding that damned hatchet and Rolland thought he was done for. The madman had pressed the blade into Rolland's back.

"You're not the one I'm here for," Hiram had hissed, spittle covering the back of Rolland's bare neck. He wondered if Hiram had rabies and was contagious. "Just do as I say, and you'll be fine."

Doing as Hiram said, Rolland gave a weak knock on the door.

"Louder," Hiram ordered, pressing the blade menacingly into his back.

Rolland gave several sharp raps on the door's glass pane, which was covered from the inside by a ruffled curtain. He hoped to hell Wesley would pull the curtain aside to see who was at the door. He could hear Wesley shuffling toward the door and wanted to cry out, to warn him, but he also did not want to die.

It took forever for Wesley to unlock the door. The blood thundered so loudly in Rolland's head he thought he would have a stroke; he wanted to vomit, thinking what lay ahead. The door swung open. Wesley's toothy smile greeted him, but it instantly faded when he saw Rolland's face.

Rolland couldn't recall what happened next, except that he was being thrown, like a rag doll, off the back stoop where he landed in a small patch of tulips blooming, their colorful red and purple globes being crushed as he fell in their midst.

He hadn't looked behind him, terrified at what he might see. Instead, he had clawed his way to his feet and run like a bat out of hell, hoping he would be fast enough. He knew what was in store for poor Wesley. He had been present when his Uncle Charlie and two other men had found what was left of Katie, Hiram's wife, after he had dismembered her before burying her remains in an old well in his corn crib.

The images and smells of that day returned to Rolland in that instant and he thought he was going to pass out, reliving the absolute terror he'd felt when he'd seen a scrap of Katie Mohler impaled on the point of the iron probe Charlie had used to locate what remained of her piecemeal corpse.

His lungs felt like they would burst. His chest was on fire. He needed to stop, to catch his breath, but he couldn't. He wouldn't. He was the only chance of survival Wesley had, and he kept running.

*****

Chapter Fifty

Wesley tried to protest, to plead, but he was dealing with someone completely insane. The hatchet swooped down. Too late, Wesley moved his hand gripping the edge of the countertop. The razor-sharp, wedge-shaped blade cropped off the top half of the little finger on Wesley's right hand. Brutally separated from its base, the finger popped into the air and, when it landed, rolled toward the canister set arranged against the back of the counter and stopped before the one marked 'tea'.

A scream of pain and fear burst from Wesley. Blood ran from his amputated finger onto the counter and floor. He lifted his arm to help staunch the flow, looking at his wound in horror. Hiram was positively gleeful about what he had done.

"Whee! Look at all the blood!" he chortled. He gave the hatchet an admiring glance, then fixed Wesley with a look that promised more to come.

"For the love of God, Hiram, please don't kill me," Wesley begged. He had backed himself into a corner between the refrigerator and countertop. There was nowhere for him to go.

Hiram smiled sweetly as he closed in on Wesley.

"You're right," Wesley gabbled. "I should've shared my mushrooms with you. There were plenty for both of us, and … and you can have them all, Hiram. They'll be up any day now. Probably some peeking up through the leaves as we speak …" he babbled.

"Mushrooms, Wes?" Hiram asked, looking astonished. "You think this is about mushrooms?" He shook his head in disbelief.

"It's not about my mushrooms?" Wesley asked, taken aback. His head was aching, his finger throbbing.

"YOUR mushrooms, Wes?" Hiram said softly. "There you go again, being greedy. You just said I could have them all, so they are MY mushrooms, Wes." Hiram's voice had crescendoed to a slight boom.

"Yes! Yes! Of course, they're all yours. That's what I meant to say, Hiram." He was part of some extra dimensional happening to which Hiram, alone, had the script. He knew his life hung by a thread, a very fine thread, which Hiram could pluck, in or out of his madness. All Wesley could hope for was to continue distracting him with conversation, but it was like talking into a tin can.

*****

The phone on Charlie's desk was ringing belligerently when he arrived at the police station early in the morning. He almost didn't answer it, but he gave in and caught it on the last ring.

"Shannon PD," he said into the receiver, "Charlie Simmons."

"This is the State Hospital over here in Lima. I need to talk to the officer in charge."

"That'd be me," Charlie replied. An uneasy feeling had seized the back of his neck and was slowly crawling its way down his torso.

"Officer Simmons, I'm Sargent O'Reilly. Sir, I'm calling from the Correctional Institute to report a prisoner escape."

"Go on, Sargent," Charlie urged. He knew what was coming.

"Prisoner number 31224, name of Hiram Mohler, is missing from the facility here in Lima and we have reason to believe he is headed your way. He is considered extremely dangerous and we urge you to be on the lookout for this prisoner and, should he be spotted, extreme caution used if you approach him."

"What makes you think he's coming toward Shannon?" Charlie asked.

"Well, Sir," Sargent O'Reilly responded, "he killed an inmate a while back and when he was put in solitary he ranted and raved to be let out. Said there was one more he had to get. We took that to mean he had some unfinished business back home. You got any idea what he meant by that, Sir?"

An image of Wes Montgomery appeared in Charlie's mind's eye. "Yes, Sargent, I do," he answered. "And I need to go, now, Sargent." He tossed the handset in the cradle, grabbed his revolver and car keys, and sped out the door.

It was still early, before people were heading to work, so the streets were fairly quiet and almost empty. That did not stop Charlie from using his siren as he roared north on Main Street in the direction of Wes Montgomery's farm. An elderly woman who lived on Riley Street, Mary Weisen, was walking her Pomeranian and, when she heard the siren, whisked her pet into the safety of her arms as Charlie sped past.

'What on earth is he about, at this hour?' she wondered. She stood, watching, until she saw him turn onto County Line Road in the distance.

A short way up on County Line Charlie saw a lone figure jogging in his direction. As he got closer, he recognized his nephew, Rolland. At the approach of the police car Rolland waved his arms to flag it down. He was bent double, trying to catch his breath, when Charlie stopped beside him.

"Rolland, what are you doing out here at this hour?" Charlie asked.

Rolland panted and huffed. "Mohler," he rasped. "He's got Wes Montgomery."

Charlie stiffened at the news. He gripped the steering wheel until his knuckles turned white.

"Get in, Rolland," he said.

Rolland shook his head. "I'm not going …"

"Get in, Rolland!" Charlie ordered. "I'm not leaving you out here alone with that madman on the loose. You're safer with me. Get in!"

Rolland stumbled to the passenger side of the cruiser, opened door, and collapsed into the front seat. Charlie put the car in gear and sped on to the Montgomery farm.

*****

Chapter Fifty-One

Hiram had escaped from the insane asylum in Lima by way of hanging on underneath the chassis of a meat delivery truck he had helped unload in the asylum's vast kitchen area. No one noticed his absence. One minute he was there, and the next minute he was gone. The busy mayhem of men milling around moving supplies covered his break.

When the truck was free of the prison and heading toward its next delivery it was stopped by the flashing lights of a railroad crossing just over a mile from the prison. Hiram disengaged, rolled out from under the truck, and casually hopped on a flatbed car on the train, riding it to Shannon. He jumped from the rail car long before it made the station as it slowly snaked its way into town. He lay low along the bank of the Riley until it grew dark, and under cover of night fall made his way to his small farm on the north side of town. He spent the night in the barn on his farm and found a change of clothes so he could get out of his prison garb. Before it got light, he stole over to the neighboring Montgomery farm. After honing a hatchet in Wes' shop, he lay in wait by the back door where, luck would have it, Rolland gave him an easy entré into Wesley's house.

*****

"Enough!" Hiram Mohler roared, swinging the deadly hatchet in a powerful arc toward Wes Montgomery's head. Wes dodged slightly to the left as the hatchet sped toward him. The dodge saved his life, but the hatchet almost sliced off a portion of Wes' scalp in its trajectory.

Not quite to the bone, but deep enough to cut a wedge from Wes' skull, the blood poured from the wound, running down Wes' face, blinding him in his left eye. A chunk of flesh and hair hung from his scalp, still attached. The grisly injury left Wes stunned, heading into shock at the trauma caused by the wound. He started to slip in and out of consciousness. He knew he did not have long to live.

That last blow from Hiram had sent Wesley to the floor in the corner. His head felt like one big throbbing balloon, ready to burst. His stomach was woozy from the pain and blood loss, and he felt increasingly disoriented. His rifle was completely out of reach, but even if he had his gun, he would not have been able to do much with it. His hands were slick with blood and his vision so impaired he would have had to use it as a club.

Hiram had become extremely agitated discussing the mushroom situation. It still galled him to no end that Wes had been so piggish with the morels. He had grown tired of the talk and lashed out with the hatchet. He figured now was the time to finish the job and head on. Maybe he would check for morels in the orchard on his way.

"Otto," Wes mumbled.

"Say what?" Hiram asked.

"Why did you kill Otto?" Wes managed.

"Water under the bridge," Hiram replied. He began pacing around the large country kitchen. He opened the refrigerator. He was hungry, all of a sudden, but found nothing that appealed to him. He flipped open a few cupboard doors with the same result. When he walked past the counter where the canisters sat and noticed the severed finger, he remembered his objective and swung round.

"No offense, Montgomery," he said, "but I've got other things to do. Let's get this over with."

Wesley wiped the blood away from his eye with the sleeve of his flannel shirt. He was gripped with the terror of what was to come. He couldn't just let Hiram butcher him like a hog for market. He would have one, and only one, chance to save himself. He reached way down inside himself for strength and clarity of mind. And he prayed. God, he prayed!

A welcome calm settled over Wesley. He felt strength build in his legs and arms. He watched Hiram closely, measuring the distance between the two men. He was as ready as he would ever be for the assault that was to come.

Hiram stood squarely in front of Wesley. At first glance he seemed to have a serene smile, but a closer look, especially at Hiram's eyes, said different. They were over-the-edge manic, hard as flint, looking from another world. The eyes said someone other than Hiram was home. Hiram's mouth suddenly contorted into a snarl. He raised the hatchet and struck at Wesley, savagely.

Wesley had been watching his insane adversary and saw the blow coming. With all the strength he could muster he heaved his body out of the corner. With his arms crossed in front of his face and neck he tried to rush Hiram's attack, thereby shortening the arc of the blow from the hatchet.

His move caught Hiram completely off guard. Hiram pulled his swing, which greatly broke its force. He didn't connect with his intended target, Wes' head. Instead, the side of the blade glanced off Wesley's wrist and sliced into the flesh of his left forearm.

The onslaught left Wesley with a broken wrist bone and a gash on his arm that bled profusely. What little strength he had left drained from him and he was left weak and rubbery. The additional loss of blood from his new injury hastened the onset of shock.

Hiram was enraged that his quarry had thwarted what he intended as the death blow.

"You'll regret that, Montgomery, by God, you will!" he roared. He lifted the weapon to deliver another blow and Wesley, too weak to sit up, toppled over, leaving his torso flat on the floor, face down, with his neck exposed.

Hiram started, but when he realized Wesley had fainted, his looney face lit up with a demented grin.

"All stretched out, just like a chicken's neck," he said. He raised the hatchet to deliver a decapitating blow. "Come to Papa," he said.

"Hold it, Hiram!" Charlie ordered.

With the door left open to the scenario in the kitchen Charlie had immediately assessed Wes' situation. He had drawn his revolver and run inside, hoping he wasn't too late.

Hiram either did not hear, or ignored, Charlie's command to stop. He was on the verge of starting a powerful down swing when Charlie's Smith & Wesson 38 spit two plugs into Hiram's back. The gun's report in the kitchen was deafening, reverberating around the walls.

For a moment, it seemed the bullets had no effect on the madman. He appeared to pause, briefly, as though considering Charlie's words, and deciding to disobey. Time seemed to stand still; Charlie wondered if his gun had been loaded with blanks. In slow motion, Hiram's now lifeless body crumbled to the kitchen floor next to where Wesley lay, unconscious. The hatchet landed next to Wesley's head with a thud, sticking in the floor's linoleum, narrowly missing its intended mark.

*****

Chapter Fifty-Two

Blanche Gruman sold her beauty salon and headed west, figuring to settle in Los Angeles. She needed a change and the City of Angels was about as different from Shannon as you could get. Who knows? With her good looks and savoir faire maybe she would end up catering to the rich and famous.

Homer Schmidt became a fixture at Shannon's Methodist Church. He more than paid back what he had pilfered over the years and increased his tithe by another five percent. Doc Steiner continued to serve Shannon's residents, and Stillman Roney kept on banking.

Pete Gaite decided Shannon was not lowkey enough for him, after all, so he moved his wife and his sister to a little farming community about a half hour from Detroit. He had never signed up for murder and blackmail. His move left the job of police chief vacant in Shannon. The city fathers were unanimous in offering the job to Charlie if he wanted it. Travis Hunt was especially insistent, calling Charlie a man of ability and discretion.

So, here he was on a fine morning in May, settling in for a piece of banana cream pie and cup of coffee at The Pine. The restaurant's front door had been propped open to let in the beautiful day.

Brrrinnngg! Brrrinnngg!

Charlie heard Molly Snook call out, ""Peg Birknauer, ew doddamned big liar, tell me a big lie!"

"No time, today, Miss Molly," Peg replied, as he pedaled by. "I gotta message to deliver to the fire chief."

Just then Sankie Fenton ran into The Pine in a high state of excitement.

"Gypsies have just left Pandora," he announced. "Word has it they're a headin' this way!"

*****

About Bluette Matthey

Bluette Matthey is a product of the melting pot of America's settlers, with her ancestry rooted in the Swiss, German, and English cultures. She is a keen reader of mysteries who loves to travel and explore, especially in Europe.

Bluette currently lives in Beziers, France, with her husband and band of loving cats.

Other books by Bluette Matthey include the Hardy Durkin Travel Mystery series:

Corsican Justice
Abruzzo Intrigue
Black Forest Reckoning
Dalmatian Traffick
Engadine Aerie

"I hope you've enjoyed **Two Murders Too Many**. I would love to hear from you, Readers. Please feel free to contact me via my website, bluematthey.com, or my email: notyourusualtrek@gmail.com.

www.ingramcontent.com/pod-product-compliance
Lightning Source LLC
Chambersburg PA
CBHW020758190726

48285CB00006B/2083